It Came from the MULTIPLEX

80s Midnight Chillers

PRAISE

"Highly recommended! In a literary tribute to 1980s slasher movies, these illustrious horror writers stay true to the genre formula: sex, drugs, rock n' roll, and scary monsters. These 14 creepy tales take place at drive-ins and movie theaters—where on-screen horrors burst into even worse horrors OFF the screen!"
—**Brinke Stevens**, actress in THE SLUMBER PARTY MASSACRE

"IT CAME FROM THE MULTIPLEX is absolutely perfect! Weird, twisted, gross, funny, terrifying. A true homage to a decade that inspired a generation of top storytellers!"
—**Jonathan Maberry**, New York Times bestselling author of V-WARS and ROT & RUIN

"These stories traverse the dark alleys of the 80s... they're the reflections of the neon bar sign in the rain puddles...they're the raw pain of a lost generation dressed in glamour and running eyeliner...they're the hidden VHS tapes at the back of the video store they warned you about—the ones you can't resist or get out of your mind after watching. This is your brain on horror. Any questions?"
— **John Palisano**, President of the Horror Writers Association, Bram Stoker Award®-Winning author of GHOST HEART

"An enjoyable horror anthology with a strong midnight chillers concept."
—**Kirkus Reviews**

"The universally well-paced, imaginative selections sizzle with energy, delivering an intoxicating blend of spine-tingling chills and 80s nostalgia."
—**Publishers Weekly**, starred review

It Came from the

MULTIPLEX

80s Midnight Chillers

Directed by Joshua Viola

STARRING

Bret & Jeanni Smith

Paul Campion

Warren Hammond

Angie Hodapp

Alvaro Zinos-Amaro

Dayton Ward

Kevin Dilmore

Betty Rocksteady

Keith Ferrell

Gary Jonas

Mario Acevedo

Orrin Grey

Sean Eads

Joshua Viola

K. Nicole Davis

Stephen Graham Jones

Steve Rasnic Tem

Kevin J. Anderson

HEX PUBLISHERS

This is a work of fiction. All characters, organizations, and events portrayed in this book are products of the authors' imaginations and/or are used fictitiously.

IT CAME FROM THE MULTIPLEX
80s MIDNIGHT CHILLERS

All stories are copyrighted to their respective authors, and used here with their permission. An extension of this copyright page can be found on the Acknowledgments page.

Edited by Joshua Viola

Produced by Bret Smith, Jeanni Smith and Joshua Viola
Copyedits by Jennifer Melzer, Bret Smith and Jeanni Smith
Cover illustrations by AJ Nazzaro
Cover design by Joshua Viola
Story illustrations by Xander Smith
Header art by Aaron Lovett
Art direction by Joshua Viola
Typesets and formatting by Dustin Carpenter

A Hex Publishers Book

Published & Distributed by Hex Publishers, LLC
PO BOX 298
Erie, CO 80516

www.HexPublishers.com

Joshua Viola, Publisher

Print ISBN-13: 978-1-7339177-5-9
eBook ISBN-13: 978-1-7339177-6-6
First Edition: September 2020
10 9 8 7 6 5 4 3 2 1
Printed in the U.S.A.

Keith Ferrell's passion for storytelling was unrivaled. He was happy to share advice as long as there was promise of friendship. Keith was part of the Hex family from the beginning and will be sorely missed. Find his work and read, read, read. But, more importantly—as Keith would say—write, write, write.

In Loving Memory:
Keith Ferrell, 1953-2020

CONTENTS

5
FOREWORD
BRET & JEANNI SMITH

11
INTRODUCTION
PAUL CAMPION

15
ALIEN PARASITES FROM OUTER SPACE
WARREN HAMMOND

35
RETURN OF THE
ALIEN PARASITES FROM OUTER SPACE
ANGIE HODAPP

57
NEGATIVE CREEP
ALVARO ZINOS-AMARO

81
HELLULOID
DAYTON WARD & KEVIN DILMORE

101
RISE, YE VERMIN!
BETTY ROCKSTEADY

119
THE CRONENBERG CONCERTO
KEITH FERRELL

139
CREATURE FEATURE
GARY JONAS

161
INVISIBLE
MARIO ACEVEDO

181
SCREEN HAUNT
ORRIN GREY

199
THE DEVIL'S REEL
SEAN EADS & JOSHUA VIOLA

231
ON THE ROCKS
K. NICOLE DAVIS

243
COMING ATTRACTIONS
STEPHEN GRAHAM JONES

259
LATE SLEEPERS
STEVE RASNIC TEM

277
SPECIAL MAKEUP
KEVIN J. ANDERSON

297
CAST AND CREW

307
ACKNOWLEDGMENTS

FOREWORD

BRET AND JEANNI SMITH

What were we thinking? Organizing a horror convention *and* working on an accompanying anthology?

Like Norman Bates said, "We all go a little mad sometimes. Haven't you?"

If you haven't, then we hope to bring you to the edge in 2020. The convention has its origins in a chance conversation among Bret Smith, Dan Crosier and Dwight Thompson in 2017, with the three of them lamenting how Colorado had no dedicated horror convention. Sure, there are the famous Starfest and MileHiCon, which includes luminaries in the horror field; but Bret, Dan and Dwight felt horror was being short-changed.

But how to rectify the situation?

Joined by Bret's wife, Jeanni, and Dwight's wife, Lisa, this committee of five engaged in a serious brain-eating—ahem, brain-*storming*—session that led to the creation of the Colorado Festival of Horror.

A love and fascination with horror rests in our hearts.

Jeanni read Poe's *Tales of Mystery and Imagination* by flashlight under cover of a blanket; Bret managed to watch *Creature from the Black Lagoon* on a small black and white screen long after his parents went to bed, with only Elvira for company. The novels of Stephen King and Dean Koontz lit up our creepy imaginations. Jeanni will never forget literally jumping up in her seat when the shark launched itself onto the boat in *Jaws*, and Bret still thinks about almost puking up his strawberry Twizzlers during the chestburster scene in *Alien*.

Poor John Hurt!

No strangers to horror, we also are not strangers to conventions and fan culture. In fact, such things are considered to be our oxygen. We went to our first *Star Trek* convention in 1983. That experience was so much fun, a respite from the working world, a place where we could share our nerd credentials with the like-minded. Conventions soon became an important part of our lives, a great way to make new friends and strengthen the bonds of family. After we had our boys, conventions helped us share our love of movies and entertainment with them and nurture their imaginations. In our retirement, fandom has become a way of life; conventions provide opportunities to travel, weekends away from the mundane, and reunions with old friends.

However, we've always felt the most important part of conventions is the chance to meet the creative minds behind our favorite stories, the warm talents who bring the stories to life. It started with seeing celebrities, but we soon developed an appreciation for the directors, the special effects people, the composers, and naturally,

the writers. In the course of attending conventions over thirty years, we also developed a fascination for the mechanics of the process. What does a convention look like behind the scenes? Who handles the hundreds of crucial details that help make a convention successful? Our curiosity got the better of us and we started volunteering at conventions in 2015, learning all about the impressive logistics and attention to detail needed to create an amazing experience for the fans.

We're convinced this background and passion will make the Colorado Festival of Horror an exciting and essential experience.

We intend this anthology to be a part of that good time.

How did it come about? Well, once again our convention background played a key role. Bret met Josh Viola, the creative force behind Hex Publishers, at a comic con several years ago. When Hex released its first horror anthology, *Nightmares Unhinged,* in 2015, Bret was impressed by the quality of the participating writers and the boldness of the collection's vision. With contributions by horror stalwarts such as Steve Rasnic Tem, Edward Bryant, Stephen Graham Jones, and Steve Alten, it was clear Josh and Hex intended to make a big statement.

Several more anthologies followed, each of equal quality and exceptional design. As we came to know Josh better through the convention circuit, we knew he shared our passion for all forms of horror. When we landed upon the idea of offering a signature horror anthology as a dark, juicy lagniappe for the attendees of the Colorado Festival of Horror, Josh was the first person we sought out for advice and assistance.

We're glad to say he was happy to oblige, and the result is now in your hands.

The stories you're about to read are organized around our desire to return to those years when a new age of horror began. Some of you are old enough to remember the anticipation of sitting in a multiplex, basking in flickering bloodshed as iconic villains like Jason and Freddy and Chucky menaced hapless teenagers on screen. We speak of course of the 1980s, that marvelous decade when the gore was enough to make you toss your cookies while the campiness kept you in stitches. There's been a nostalgia for the 80s, as the success of *Stranger Things* will attest. Even more telling is the latest season of *American Horror* Story, subtitled *1984*, which pays loving tribute to classics like *Friday the 13th* and *Sleepaway Camp*.

Don't say we're just trying to capture the zeitgeist.

We've been *breathing* it all along.

Thanks to Josh and his impressive contacts in the community of literary horror, we have fourteen stories from sixteen brilliant minds who captured our theme to a tee. But anthologies—particularly horror anthologies—are more than just stories. The final element is

the right sort of artwork, something with eye-gouging, wait, eye-*popping* colors.

Fittingly, at yet another convention, Josh introduced us to AJ Nazzaro, a popular Blizzard Entertainment artist known for his work on the game *Hearthstone*. His art, his style, and his palette were perfect for *It Came from the Multiplex*. Take a moment right now to step away from this introduction and appreciate the cover. AJ brought all of his impressive skills to bear. Don't you just love the 80s girl with her 3D glasses? Don't the theater seats and popcorn put you into the scene and make you anticipate the next big scare? They sure do for us. Then you will notice individual story art throughout this anthology. We're so proud to acknowledge the work of our son, Xander Smith, who began his career as a concept artist in Hollywood by working on *Scream Queens* and *American Horror Story*.

We guess hauling him off to all of those conventions when he was little made quite the impression on him!

Last, you'll find the unique header art at the top of each page. Go ahead and flip the pages and bear witness to an animated flipbook sequence by Hex artist Aaron Lovett, whose work has appeared in *Spectrum* and was licensed by AMC for *Fear the Walking Dead*.

Quite the collaboration, yes?

We hope the stories in this anthology will make an equally positive impression on you. We now leave you in the care of fourteen chilling tales from local, national and international authors, some of whom are Bram Stoker Award winners. Here you will find were-wolves and ghosts, psychos and serial killers, eldritch monsters and bug infestations, the terrifying unknown and the devil incarnate. You will be shocked, surprised, scared and maybe even amused while you devour this collection of short stories.

So turn the page and immerse yourself in our favorite bloody decade. Let your imagination be chased down the aisles of your favorite multiplex.

Caveat Lector.

Bret and Jeanni Smith
January 2020

INTRODUCTION

PAUL CAMPION

Horror pictures have always been central to my life. As a child in the 70s, I was lucky enough to have parents who let me stay up late and watch those scary black-and-white movies on TV. But it wasn't until I was a teenager and old enough to go to the cinema without my parents tagging along that I truly discovered the joy of the horror film experience. Sharing the vicarious rush of mayhem and terror with an audience of like-minded thrill-seekers evolved into a calling that lead me to a career in the film industry and the opportunity to create cinematic monsters of my own.

The stories in this anthology are a love letter to the 80s, the golden age of horror where blood and gore were faithfully rendered in 35mm Technicolor. It was a glorious time to experience films like *Re-Animator, The Thing, Hellraiser, The Lost Boys, Prince of Darkness, Children of the Corn,* and many, many more.

Today, what most people seem to forget is that the film experience isn't just about watching movies, it's also about *where* you watch them. A pristine theater can't provide the right ambience to stoke a ghoulish adventure. You need texture and atmosphere, and the seedier the playhouse, the better. The 80s was chock-full of such places.

In 1981, I drove to a fleapit cinema in South East London in my first car, a Volkswagen Beetle (and take note, beetles and insects are important in what you're about to read) to see an over-the-top horror flick I'd heard about called *The Evil Dead*. Back then, all of our news about upcoming films came from movie trailers on rented video cassettes or from magazines like *Starburst*, *Cinefantastique*, and *Fangoria*.

The cinema in question was on the verge of being condemned or torn down. The threadbare carpet was sticky from God knows what (it had previously been a porno house), the screen was tattered and slack, and the toilets were best avoided. But all its crumbling shabbiness made the perfect backdrop for a crowd yearning to scream, howl, and laugh at the madness Sam Raimi, Rob Tapert, and Bruce Campbell unleashed upon them. People leapt to their feet, shrieking in fright, the calamity exaggerated by the disturbing creak and bang of ancient fold-up seats.

There's an irony about the stories of *Multiplex* set in and around movie theaters. In these pages, the safe places we used to visit for entertainment have become venues of horror that devour the unsuspecting. As a child, I loved Saturday night movie screenings, but in Sean Eads and Joshua Viola's "The Devil's Reel", a Christian youth group's matinee becomes anything but a holy sanctuary. In Gary Jonas' tale, "Creature

Feature", a deserted cinema harbors flesh-eating patrons not of this earth, alluding to gruesome images from *Gremlins*.

Indoor theaters were not the only place to watch a movie in the 80s, and in *Multiplex*, drive-ins also get their due. In Mario Acevedo's "Invisible", a serial killer stalks his prey in such a location, taking full advantage of the night sky. In Warren Hammond and Angie Hodapp's double-feature, a drive-in becomes refuge to a giant, monstrous threat, offered as an homage to bygone classics from the 50s such as *Them!*, *Tarantula!*, and *The Deadly Mantis*.

Which brings me back to insects. There are a lot of them in what you're about to read. Those repulsive buggers, hiding in the dark, waiting for the lights to go out...

Growing up in England, cockroaches weren't something I'd ever encountered. Back then, the closest I got to knowing what they were like was watching that *Creepshow* episode "They're Creeping Up on You!". I remember the joy and disgust I felt when the roaches burst out of Upson Pratt's corpse. Apparently, over 20,000 cockroaches were used when filming, many of which escaped into the building where their offspring are probably still there to this day. Waiting.

I recently moved to Auckland, New Zealand, and for the first time in my life I'm living in a subtropical climate, which means I'm dealing with cockroaches. They're everywhere in the house; the bedroom, the bathroom, the kitchen, and occasionally scuttling down my office wall even as I'm typing this up. Spraying, trapping, and flushing their squirming bodies down the toilet is my new normal. After reading these stories, my overactive brain wonders if the roaches hiding in my garden are preparing to amass and infiltrate the house through a window carelessly left open, just like the horde in *Creepshow*. Maybe I'd be better off in a movie theater. Then again, if these stories have anything to say, maybe not.

To a cinephile, the cinema is our cathedral, our church, but like many churches, our places of worship have been forgotten, unappreciated by new generations who prefer the sedentary convenience of watching movies on a mobile phone or laptop. Think of how many stories have played out over the decades in those abandoned theaters, both on and off screen. So much history must surely have left a grisly residue, and *Multiplex* will give you an idea of what may be lurking inside, should you dare to look.

ALIEN PARASITES FROM OUTER SPACE

WARREN HAMMOND

ALIEN PARASITES FROM OUTER SPACE

WARREN HAMMOND

Moths swarm the hot-pink neon of the Meteor Drive-In marquee as Carl Cramer pedals past. The long driveway leads steeply downhill, and Carl lets the bike pick up speed, the rush of July air cooling his sweaty face. He brakes as the hill levels out and stops at the ticket booth. He pulls a five from the pocket of his no-name jeans and hands it to Scar-y Joe. Not *scary*, though most wouldn't hesitate to use that word to describe Joe. It's *scar*-y, as in burns all over his face.

Joe hands back three singles. "It's a good one tonight," he says. "A classic."

Carl pockets his change. "Is it true about the director?"

Joe nods. His head is a splotchy patchwork of hair and scar tissue. Some say he was in a fiery car crash. Others say it happened in Vietnam. Nobody seems to know which. "Directed by Jasper Reid," he says. "Born and raised right here in Janesburg, Nebraska."

"Did you know him?"

"I did. Best of friends for a time."

A car horn makes Carl jump. A Ford pickup has pulled in behind him, headlights blinding. "Hurry up, Cramer," shouts a male voice.

Andy Demps.

Carl raises a middle finger and mouths a silent *fuck you*. It's not the smartest move, but at the moment, he doesn't care how hard that two-hundred-and-seventy-pound asshole can punch. The sooner Andy leaves town to play O-line for the Huskers, the better.

He's somewhat surprised and more than a little relieved to see the truck's door stay closed. Carl shades his eyes, but the headlights are too bright to gauge Andy's reaction.

Scar-y Joe, though, he thinks this is hilarious. His laugh is more of a cackle, his shoulders bouncing up and down with each snicker.

The truck lunges forward, and a startled Carl releases his ten-speed and jumps aside, though he knows immediately it's a feint. The Ford has moved only a foot forward, and Carl hears laughter from inside.

Feeling the flush in his cheeks, Carl snatches his bike and pedals through the gate into the flat-bottomed crater where the Meteor Drive-in resides. It was a big attraction thirty years ago, just like the Meteor Mini Putt, the Meteor Motel, and the Crater Slide. That was before I-80 was built. Before all the cross-country traffic was drawn away from town.

Only the drive-in still operates—in July and August— and based on the weed-chewed pavement, Carl isn't sure it will survive to see '87. He steers clear of potholes and broken glass until he finds space number fifty-

three, the one with the ratty folding chair propped against the post. He drops the kickstand, positions the chair next to his bike, and grabs the speaker from its post to hang it from the Schwinn's crossbar.

Headlights approach, and he prays it's not who he thinks it is. But of course, it's Andy's growling Ford. The truck backs into space fifty-four to share the same speaker pole. Andy gets out of the truck, and from the opposite side comes fellow offensive lineman Wade Spratt. A third person slides out from the middle seat: Becca Cline. She wears a tight pair of Jordaches, a green tee, and Andy's well-worn Nebraska cap.

She reaches back into the cab to grab a six-pack of Bartles & Jaymes wine coolers. She smiles at Carl, "Want one?"

Carl shakes his head.

"Are you sure? They're Body Shot Lime flavor."

Again, he declines.

The three of them climb up into the bed of the truck and sit facing the screen, backs against the cab. He should be glad she's here. Her presence will have a dampening effect on Andy and Wade's worst testosterone-jacked impulses. But seeing her wearing Andy's cap still stings. Carl knows how stupid it is to feel that way. Despite being in the same classes all of their lives, Becca has never once showed the least bit of interest in him, but that hasn't stopped him from imagining what could be if he wasn't so...*weird*.

He doesn't like that word, especially when applying it to himself. But he can't escape it. Might as well have it tattooed on his forehead, if it weren't already so painfully obvious from the mom-cut hair and the generic swoosh-free sneakers. He long since realized he couldn't change the way he was, and he learned to accept it. What he can't understand is why his classmates can't accept it too. Why can't they just leave him be? Is it really so strange that a person doesn't like baseball or basketball or any other kind of ball? So what if he prefers to play Dungeons & Dragons all by himself? Why does anybody care if all of his notebooks are filled with sketches of swords and war hammers and labyrinthine dungeon plans?

About the only normal thing he does is watch movies, though he knows his tastes run toward the, well, *weird*. The VCR he bought with his own money is his most prized possession, and the after-school job he works at Janesburg Videos gives him access to thousands of films. His favorites are the videotapes that don't come in perfectly produced boxes. He likes the ones that show up in their original Memorex or Maxell sleeves and are only identifiable by crooked or peeling stickers on the black plastic spines. Ones with titles like *Swamp Tramp of the Underworld* and *Fanged Hamster Slumber Party.*

That is what makes tonight's feature so special. The movie never made it to TV or VHS or any other format beyond its initial release in the late 60s. Viewings

are so rare many around town insist the movie never really existed.

The projector fires up to bathe the screen in bright white light. Several of the screen's panels are missing, and those that remain are warped badly enough to create a visible crosshatch of seams. Hundreds of moths dart and dance in the projector's beam, casting dancing black dots on the blank screen.

Carl sits forward as the first shot appears. It's a crow sitting on a fence, a cornfield in the background. He thinks he recognizes the grain silo as the same one five miles north. The crow caws, and the movie's title appears in big purple letters: *Alien Parasites from Outer Space*. Carl smiles and claps until he realizes he is the only one applauding. A Budweiser bottle cap lands near his feet. "Keep it down, Cramer."

Carl hears a banging sound and turns to see that Scar-y Joe has moved from the ticket booth to opening the concession window. Carl double-times for it before a line forms. If he's fast, he can be back before the opening credits finish.

By the time Carl arrives, Scar-y Joe has already filled a double-meteor-sized cup with root beer. He tops the soda with a plastic lid and hands over a king-size box of Junior Mints. Carl notices the Walkman headphones sitting askew on Scar-y Joe's nubby ears but has no interest in asking what he's listening to. Other than movie scores, music holds little interest to Carl. He pays up, then nabs a straw and a long plastic spoon before spinning back around to face the screen.

The credits are over, and a pair of teenagers are walking through a cornfield. Carl hustles back to his spot and drops into his chair. The girl is wearing a poodle skirt, and the boy reminds Carl of the Fonz. They're carrying a blanket and speaking in hushed tones about finding a quiet, secluded place near the creek.

The scene makes a sudden cut. The background is now black but dotted with pinpricks of light. A starfield. The camera pans left to land on a planet the color of Welch's Grape Juice. Another planet swings into view, and the two orbs collide like those Clackers toys. The view cuts to an explosion. A slo-mo spray of rocks, dirt, and sparks hurls toward the lens. Next, the camera focuses on one particular flying rock that dangles from a barely visible wire.

Andy is laughing now. "Holy shit, that is so fake!"

Carl resists the urge to shush. The movie cuts to show Earth. Then the rock. The music picks up pace as the view switches back to Earth. Then the rock. Earth. Rock.

Back to the teens in the cornfield. They look up at the sky, and the movie freezes on terrified faces for several seconds before the film becomes overexposed, the colors saturating into a blur. The speaker hanging on Carl's ten-speed spits and crackles over the sound of a bomb going off.

Carl is nodding his head. This movie kicks ass! As is his routine, he sucks his straw until he's downed a third of his root beer and pulls the lid open. He sets the open cup on the ground before grabbing the box of Junior Mints in both fists so he can strangle the life out of it. He likes his mints mushy. He wrings the box a few more times, then opens it and uses the spoon to scoop the melty mash into his root beer.

A moth bumps his forehead, and he swipes it away before digging the spoon into his cup. He fishes out a minty mass and gleefully gobbles it down.

The movie is starting to drag now. It's ten years later, and the town has rebuilt. Two high school seniors—Stan and Sam—hog the screen time. Stan's parents are going out of town, and the boys scheme to throw the biggest, baddest party in the history of parties. Typical high school fare.

A scream startles Carl, but it doesn't come from the speaker. "Fuckin' moths," says Becca. "It flew in my ear."

Andy and Wade laugh, and another bottle cap arcs from the truck.

On the screen, Stan is handing out invites to the party. He goes into the library and pins one to the bulletin board. He hears a sound. Spooky music starts as Stan creeps between the bookshelves. He rounds a corner, and his eyes go wide with shock. The librarian is there, looking how a movie librarian should look. Glasses. Pinned-up hair. Black ankle-length skirt. Except this librarian is completely topless. "Oh, Stan, I'm sorry I didn't hear you come in," she says with a flirty batting of the eyes.

"Woohoo! Now we're talking!" shouts Andy. "Why aren't you clapping, Cramer?"

This kind of random encounter happens in a lot of the movies Carl watches. He's never been a fan of such scenes. Stuff like that just doesn't seem as realistic as the rest of it.

Carl bobs for more mints, and more bottle caps bounce on the pavement until the movie finally advances to party night. Stan's farmhouse sits dramatically on the edge of the crater. Carl recognizes the two-story wooden farmhouse as belonging to the Fullers. It was one of the many places his mother used to clean before her back got too bad.

Stan and Sam are in the kitchen spiking a bowl of punch. It's not the same kitchen Carl's mother used to scrub. Based on the stucco walls and Spanish tile, the interior shots were done somewhere in southern California. That doesn't bother Carl at all. He knows a movie as great as this one can't be judged by such details. Something serious bubbles under the surface of the story. Something in the subtext. He knows it's there, though he can't quite put his finger on it.

"How's the summer treating you, Carl?"

Carl is slow to notice the voice. When he pulls his eyes from the screen, Becca Cline is standing right next

to him, a box of popcorn in her hand. He didn't even notice her going to the concession window.

"It's a hot one," he says.

She tilts her head. "Hot one?"

"The summer. You asked about the summer."

"I asked about *you*," she says. "Still working at the video store?"

He nods. He can't remember the last time she talked to him. "I work in the back most days, but if you ask for me, I can find the best movies for you. Ever seen *Trout Rodeo?* It's a good one."

Before she can respond, Wade shouts, "Show us your tits!" at the newest brunette on screen. Andy laughs hysterically. The shouts of *keep it down* accompanied by irritated honking only makes him laugh harder and louder.

Becca shakes her head. "Classy, aren't they?"

Carl figures silence is enough of an answer.

Becca takes off Andy's cap, curls the bill, and shoves it in the back pocket of her Jordaches. "Some days, I really have to wonder what I'm doing. Hey, you're friendly with Scar-y Joe, aren't you?"

Carl shrugs his shoulders.

"I mean you come here every week, right? You probably know him better than anybody."

"Maybe," admits Carl.

"Did you see his headphones?"

Carl nods.

"They're not plugged into anything. The cord is just dangling."

"So?"

"Isn't that weird? I was curious to see what he was listening to but I didn't see his Walkman. The cord runs to nowhere."

Carl swats at another moth. "I guess that is strange."

"Ever notice how nobody ever talks about him? My parents, they'll talk about what a shame it is he turned out like he did, but they never say what actually happened."

"Maybe they don't know."

She rolls her eyes. "Please. You can't fart behind a tree without everybody in town knowing about it. Anyway, good talking to you."

"Same here," he says, though what he wishes he could say is, "Don't leave."

Using the back tire as a step-stool, she climbs into the truck.

Carl's eyes turn to the screen. The party is in full swing now. A reverbed guitar blares through the speakers, and the camera zooms in and out before turning upside down—the director's way of saying, *Rockin' party.*

The view cuts to a girl, topless, of course, and in bed with Sam. Her name is Mimi, and she and Sam pass a joint back and forth while saying things like *groovy* and *far out.* Suddenly annoyed, Mimi jams a finger in

her ear. A concerned Sam asks what's the matter, and she whines that it itches.

The camera zooms way in, so close all you can see is finger and ear and hair. A vaudevillian sound effect whistles through the speaker, and the view zooms back out. "It's better now," she says in a dull monotone.

Somebody knocks on the door, and she answers it, naked.

It's another girl, a cheerleader who has shown up in several of the previous scenes. Mimi stabs her in the chest, and the cheerleader collapses.

"No way!" shouts Andy. "You saw her, she didn't have a knife a second ago."

Carl tunes Andy out. He's starting to understand what's going on. The teens in this movie, it's like some of them are possessed. Not in control of themselves. The alien parasites that rode that meteor to Earth must enter through the ear. That itching sensation is them breaking through and latching onto the brain.

One of the kids goes Van Gogh and slices off an ear. Another boy fires up a John Deere and runs over a pair of lovers. This movie is so awesome!

Still, the party continues. Andy grumbles about how Sam and Stan seem oblivious to what's going on. "He watched his girlfriend kill the cheerleader, and he's acting like nothing happened," he says. True to form,

Sam keeps cranking the Hi-Fi and adding more spike to the punch.

The scene cuts to town. The sheriff is at his desk, and the phone rings. He's an actor, of course, but the police station is the real one on the corner of Walnut and Shade. The sheriff picks up and gets an earful from a panicked teen, but Carl doesn't hear a word of it. His jaw is dropped and his root beer is in danger of slipping through his fingers.

In the background is a maid. She empties a trash can and rests a hand on her belly.

"Isn't that your mom, Cramer?" calls Andy.

It is, and inside the rounded belly is Carl himself. He can't speak as a cold chill falls over him. This isn't a coincidence. He knows it down in his core. Jasper Reid, the director, did this on purpose. He knew Carl would be watching one day.

The message is unmistakable. Incontrovertible.

That is *his* mom. That is *him* in her belly.

On screen, more murders plague the house party. The beheading by scythe would be Carl's favorite, but he's not paying attention. Instead, he sips absently at his fizzy, mint-chocolatey root beer, and scans the area. He sees dozens of cars and trucks. He sees Scar-y Joe refilling the popcorn popper.

It's too dark to see the crater walls, but he can see where their black shadows meet the stars above, and he shivers. All might look normal, but he knows the parasites are here. Right here in this very crater. Their home world was destroyed, and a piece of it slammed into Earth and is still buried somewhere under Carl's chair.

A pink projectile lands by his feet. He jumps from his seat before realizing it's a piece of paper folded into a tight wad. He picks it up and unfolds the note.

Meet me in the bathroom in ten minutes. Something weird is going on. —B

He looks at her and mouths *why me?*

She rolls her eyes and jerks a thumb at Andy, who is trying to open a Bud bottle with his eye socket. All he succeeds at is opening the skin over his eyelid.

He nods. *Okay, ten minutes.*

Turning back to the screen, Carl decides he better start paying attention or he might miss the message the moviemaker is trying to convey to him. He wonders for a moment if he might be crazy, but immediately dismisses it. If the Beatles sent messages to Charlie Manson on *The White Album*, then why can't Jasper Reid be sending messages to Carl?

Another girl on the screen scratches at her ear before the whistle lets us know she's been taken. The scene cuts to a drunk Stan, but the sound of a chainsaw sobers him. He's in a tool shed, and the buzz of the chainsaw is coming from somewhere outside. He slips under a bench as the shed door slides open. From his hiding place, he sees long legs and white go-go boots.

"What the fuck?" asks Andy. "That girl was wearing overalls a minute ago."

Idiot. Ever occur to him that the farm girl might have go-go boots under her overalls? Clearly, Andy isn't sophisticated enough to appreciate the art of a movie like this one.

The chainsaw is visible, smoke drifting from its orange casing. Stan is shaking. He covers his mouth to keep from screaming. The go-go boots clop softly on the wood floor, little puffs of dust kicking up with each footfall. A gas can sits on the floor, and she tips it over. Gasoline puddles across the floor.

"Convenient that the can wasn't capped," says Wade.

Go-go chainsaw girl exits the shed and tosses a match before locking the door.

The shed goes up quick, and Carl is riveted to find out how Stan will escape this one. Except he doesn't escape. Not until the shed collapses. Only then does a figure run free, his entire body engulfed in flame.

Carl looks at the concession stand. Scar-y Joe is there, but he's covering his eyes so he can't see the screen. Is that how it happened, Joe? Or should I say Stan?

From the truck, Becca Cline is staring at him, her eyebrows raised as if to say, *Are we meeting or what?*

Carl walks to the restroom, pushes open the door labeled *Girls* in Magic Marker. "Anybody in here?" he calls to make sure it's vacant.

He goes to the sink and opens the tap. He fills cupped hands with water and splashes his face. Becca Cline will be here any second, and he needs to be ready.

He can't believe she wants to talk to him. Of all people, she chose *him*. His heart should be soaring right now. Finally, after all these years, she can see Andy for

the shallow, self-centered jerk he is. Her alarm bells are going off, and in this time of need, she is spurning the big, bad football player to run into the arms of the weird kid.

But Carl knows deep down it's all a ruse. A setup. He's too weird for someone like her. It's the way things are, and it's never going to change.

He hurries into one of the stalls and lifts the heavy porcelain lid from the toilet's tank. Hugging the weighty ceramic slab, he posts himself alongside the bathroom door. His heart is chugging like a runaway train, and he's sucking air like he's just pedaled up the crater wall.

The door cracks open. "Carl, are you in here?"

His voice cracks, but he manages an affirmative.

She pushes her way into the bathroom. Carl steps behind her. Her hair is pulled into a ponytail, and Andy's cap sticks out from her back pocket.

He wishes he didn't have to do this, but he knows it has to be done. Alien parasites are serious business. Carl swings the porcelain lid as hard as he can. It thuds into her skull, and she drops. Her eyes are still open, but they're lost. Swimming.

"Sorry, Becca," he says. "I know you're one of them."

Blood pools on the floor. Becca's mouth opens and closes soundlessly. Carl can't tell if she understands what's happening to her.

Headlights peak through the cracked door, and Carl throws his body against it. The movie is over, and cars are leaving. Somebody might decide to stop at the restroom before departing.

He watches Becca as he presses against the door. She's trying but failing to sit up. He knows he has to finish the job, but he's afraid to leave the door. He's proven right when he feels somebody pushing from the other side. "Out of order!" he shouts.

How long does he have before Andy and Wade come looking?

He stays where he is. Becca is bleeding badly, and all he wants to do is hold her, tell her it will be okay.

It's not too late to race to a phone and call for help. But he doesn't move. She's been taken. She lured Carl in here so she could kill him. There's no telling how many people she would've murdered next. Though nobody will ever know it, he knows he's a hero. He lets this fact buoy his spirit.

He hears voices outside. It's Andy and Wade, and they're talking to somebody right outside the door. The third person tells them Becca left. He says she told him to tell them her Dad came to pick her up.

Becca is lying flat now, her eyelids fluttering.

A knock sounds behind him. "They're gone," says Joe. "You can open up."

Carl pulls open the door, and Scar-y Joe waits with an icepick in hand. Painted by red neon from the concession stand, his scars look fresh.

"It went in her ear," says Carl. "She thought it was

a moth. It took control of her before she asked me to meet her here."

Joe adjusts his disconnected headphones. "That's why I wear protection. Which ear did it go in?"

"Not sure."

He drops on her quickly and stabs the icepick into her right ear. He jerks the handle around like it's a gear-shift before doing the other ear. "Fuckin' parasites. They come out every ten years."

A tear comes to Carl's eye as the last of her life drains onto the linoleum.

"You get on home now," says Joe. "I can take it from here."

Carl nabs Andy's cap. He's not sure why.

"You done good, kid," says Joe. "See you next week?"

"What's next week?"

Joe washes the blade in the sink before going to the closet to roll out a mop bucket. "The sequel."

RETURN OF THE ALIEN PARASITES FROM OUTER SPACE

ANGIE HODAPP

RETURN OF THE ALIEN PARASITES FROM OUTER SPACE

ANGIE HODAPP

The night Carl kills Becca Cline, he doesn't sleep. Not even a wink. He lies awake until dawn, and then all of the next day. He calls in sick for his shift at the video store. All he can do is stare at the movie posters on his ceiling. They advertise some of his favorites: *Millipede Hell Demons* and *Insatiable Slime Varmints* and *Tick-Tock Taxidermist*. He has always liked those movies but he knows they're just movies. Now everything is different. If *Alien Parasites from Outer Space* is real, what else is real?

He shudders, remembering how it felt to swing the toilet-tank lid at Becca's head. The sound of her head hitting the floor. Her blood oozing across the dirty tile. Her eyelids fluttering and the soft moans she made as she lay dying.

Then he remembers Scar-y Joe and the icepick and...

Carl mashes his pillow over his face. He can almost talk himself into believing it was Joe, not him, who killed Becca. But he knows she would have died anyway. All Joe did is make sure the parasite in her ear died, too.

Carl shoots to his feet and dresses quickly, then throws a few things into his backpack: a flashlight, some matches, an extra pair of headphones, and, for reasons unknown, Andy Demps' Nebraska cap—the one Becca was wearing last night. The sun is setting, but he can't hide in his room anymore pretending the alien parasites aren't out there right now infecting the people of Janesburg. He needs a plan. He needs answers.

He needs to find Scar-y Joe.

He's coasting down the driveway on his bike, headphones over his ears, cord jack dangling free, before he realizes he doesn't know where Joe lives. He pedals toward town, figuring he has to start somewhere. He has to see the second alien parasites movie tonight. The first one showed how the parasites got here, how they infect their hosts, and how their hosts turn into killing machines. The sequel, he guesses, *he hopes*, will show him how to wipe out the parasites before they can kill anyone else. Now that Joe knows Carl's in on the secret, Carl thinks maybe they can work together.

He pedals down Main Street, not sure what he's looking for. He loops around behind the video store so the manager won't see him—he's supposed to be home sick, after all—then turns onto Walnut. He brakes hard. Becca's parents' Jeep Cherokee sits in front of the police station. Through the window, Carl sees Becca's mom sobbing into a handkerchief. Her dad paces the floor. The police chief goes back and forth between them, asking questions and writing down the answers.

It's coming up on twenty-four hours since Becca was last seen, Carl realizes. Her parents are filing a missing-persons report.

The sun dips below the horizon, and a bruise-colored dusk falls over the town. A hot, July breeze stirs up the sound of rustling paper. Carl turns toward a nearby telephone pole, where a dozen posters have been thumbtacked and stapled. They're Xeroxed photographs of faces, and every one of them says MISSING or LAST SEEN or HAVE YOU SEEN ME?

Carl's blood goes cold. He recognizes Mrs. Holtz, his second-grade teacher. Mr. Barringer, the organist at St. Bart's. Little Sally Siebert, the eight-year-old sister of one of his classmates. And there, front and center, is Becca Cline, smiling at him exactly the same way she smiled at him last night. Carl figures some of the missing are hosts; others were killed by hosts. Either way, things are going to get a whole lot worse for Janesburg before they get better. The parasites have been busy, and they're just getting started.

One by one, the streetlamps along Walnut blink on. A moth bounces off Carl's cheek. He squeals and swats at the air before slapping his hands over his ears. The headphones are still in place. He looks up. Hundreds of moths swarm every streetlamp.

"Screw you!" he shouts. Are they all alien parasites or just some of them? He flips his bike around. There's no time to look for Joe. He hunches over his handlebars and pedals hard toward the Meteor Drive-In.

After a breakneck descent into the crater, he finds the cattle gate at the entrance chained and padlocked, just like every Sunday. But taped to the gate is a cardboard sign that says in blocky Magic Marker letters CLOSED FOR THE SEASON.

For the *season*? Carl sweats and shakes, and not because he just biked his fastest three miles ever. How could Joe leave him hanging like this? What could have happened in the last twenty-four hours to make Joe suddenly decide to close the drive-in for the rest of the summer?

He shimmies under the gate, then hustles toward the concession stand and leans against its cool concrete exterior, chest heaving. He listens. It's quiet here. Maybe too quiet.

It's dark, too, but Carl's afraid to use his flashlight. Light attracts moths.

He creeps toward the front of the building and peeks around the corner. Something hard smashes into his nose. White-hot pain explodes across his face, and he lands on his ass in the dirt.

"Returning to the scene of the crime, Cramer?" says the voice of Andy Demps. "What the hell'd you and Scar-y Joe do to Becca? Where is she?"

Blood streams from Carl's nose over his lips and down his chin. He rolls to his hip and spits.

"I asked you a question, Cramer. Scar-y Joe said Becca's dad came to pick her up last night, but he didn't, and Wade says he saw you go into the girls' bathroom right before Becca said she had to pee. What are you, some kind of pervert? You and that scar-faced freak snatched her from the bathroom, didn't you? And now you have her tied up somewhere. Tell me where she is or I'll rip your balls off."

"It wasn't like that. You gotta trust me." Carl squints up at Andy, the pain in his face settling into a dull throb that's worse than the punch itself.

Andy swats at the air and mutters, "Fucking moths."

Shit. Carl shrugs out of his backpack, unzips it, and digs out the extra headphones. "Put these on."

"What?" He swats again.

"Put the damn headphones on, Andy, or one of those moths is going to fly into your ear and you're going to end up like Becca."

Andy stares down at Carl. Then slowly, to Carl's surprise, he takes the headphones and fits them over his ears. When he speaks again, his voice is dangerously low. "What do you mean, end up like Becca?"

Carl knows he can't hit Andy with too much truth right now or he'll end up getting punched again. Eyes watering, he wipes his bloodied nose with the back of his hand. "I don't know where Becca is." Not a lie.

He doesn't know what Scar-y Joe did with her body. "I came here to get some answers. Are you with me?"

Andy stares, his expression twitching from confusion and disgust to fear and resignation. Finally, he offers Carl a hand. Carl takes it and lets Andy pull him to his feet.

"Lead the way, Weirdo."

Carl slings his backpack over his shoulder and moves along the front of the concession stand. He rattles the aluminum shutter that's rolled down over the service window, but it's locked tight. "Let's check out the Dumpster."

"Why the hell do you think Becca's in the Dumpster?"

Carl doesn't answer, but there's a smell in the air now, a smell that's more than trash. A smell that's getting stronger the closer they get to the Dumpster. He swallows and keeps moving.

He peeks around the corner. There in the moonlight, sitting with his back against the Dumpster, is Scar-y Joe.

"Is he dead?" Andy says.

Heart hammering, Carl pulls his flashlight from his backpack. He has no choice. He'll only use it for a couple of seconds, not long enough to attract many moths. He switches it on and aims it at Joe.

Carl hasn't eaten all day, but that doesn't stop his gut from bucking. Behind him, Andy lets out a string of cuss words.

Scar-y Joe is dead. His chin is slumped to his chest. Blood cakes the side of his face. It came from his ear, Carl realizes, so much of it that his shoulder and one

side of his wife-beater got drenched. In one hand, Scar-y Joe clutches a bloody ice pick.

"Did he do that to himself?" Andy's voice goes soprano. "Jesus, why the hell would he do that to himself?"

"He got a moth in his ear. A parasite. He knew he had to kill it before it made him kill other people." The CLOSED FOR THE SEASON sign up on the cattle gate means after Joe realized he'd been infected, the first thing he did was try to keep people away from here, away from Alien Parasite Ground Zero. Then he killed himself to protect others from his parasite's murderous urges. In Carl's book, that made Scar-y Joe a damn hero.

"You mean like in the movie last night?" Andy says. "That's crazy, Cramer. That was just a movie."

"No, it was a warning. Joe told me the parasites come out every ten years and turn people into mindless killers. Those two guys in the movie, Stan and Sam? Stan is Joe, and Sam is Jasper Reid, the director. Jasper made the movie to document what happened to them in high school and warn people that it would happen again."

Andy claps his hands over the headphones on his ears. "Is that what happened to Becca?"

Carl swallows. "Try not to think about that right now."

"What do we do?"

"There's a sequel. We have to watch it so we know how to fight back." Carl switches off the flashlight. Holding his breath, he crouches and unclips Joe's key ring from his belt.

"There's something in his other ear," Andy says.

Sure enough, shining white in the moonlight, a softball-sized thing balloons out of Scar-y Joe's unbloodied ear.

"Egg sac." Carl shivers. "Get a stick."

"We're at the bottom of a crater. There aren't any sticks down here."

"Then grab the ice pick." Carl feels around inside his backpack for his matches.

"Why do I have to?"

"Forget it. I'll do it." A surge of pleasure bolsters Carl's confidence. Andy Demps, pride of Janesburg High's offensive line, is a squeamish sissy. Realizing this, and realizing Andy knows Carl knows it, almost makes getting sucker punched worth it.

Carl takes the ice pick and gently pokes at the egg sac. He's careful not to puncture it. Who knows how many baby alien parasites are in there and what growth stage they're in? He pokes harder. Hard to say how far in it goes, but it feels rooted pretty deep. A couple more pokes and a little levering, and the sac pulls loose. It bounces off Joe's shoulder, trailing bloody, fibrous tendrils, and lands in the dirt. Carl lights a match and throws it on the sac. It goes up fast, emitting a high-pitched screech—the collective death wail of its tiny inhabitants. Carl keeps throwing lit matches until it's nothing but ashes. Three matches left. He slips them

into the back pocket of his jeans.

Andy steps past Carl and stomps on the ashes.

"Gee, Andy, good thing you're here."

"Shut up," Andy mumbles.

"Come on. Let's find the sequel."

The boys jog toward the corrugated metal shack that serves as the Meteor's projection booth. Carl flips the keys on Joe's ring, fumbling through several in the dark before he finds the right one. The lock clicks, and the door swings open.

Carl waits for Andy to close the door before switching on his flashlight. The projector sits in the center of the room. Along the walls are crooked stacks of film-reel canisters. Hundreds and hundreds of them, titles scrawled in blue marker on yellowed strips of masking tape. Carl's heart sinks. This is going to take forever. They don't have forever. Right now, the parasites are out there infecting the people of Janesburg, and they have to be stopped.

Andy grabs one of the canisters. "*Jungle Brides of the Zulu Zombie King*. Is this shit for real? What are we looking for anyway?"

"Look for anything with *alien* or *parasite* or *outer space* in the title." He props the flashlight against the projector so its beam points straight up, making the whole shack evenly dim. Looking around, he spies a stack of old, rusty reels that aren't in canisters. The film is old. Really old. *Celluloid* old.

"Damn, Joe."

Andy jumps. "What is it? What'd you find?"

"Fire hazard." Carl shakes his head at Joe's carelessness. It's a marvel those reels didn't spontaneously combust decades ago. Everyone at the video store knew Joe was a vintage film collector, but apparently the guy didn't care much about preservation. Or safety.

Carl starts flipping through a stack of canisters. He's only five or six deep when Andy shouts, "I found it!" He holds up a canister like it's a WWF championship belt. "*Queen of the Alien Parasites from Outer Space*!"

"Fuck."

Andy gloats. "Mad I found it before you?"

"No, moron. There's a *queen*."

"Oh. Yeah, that sounds bad."

Carl tosses Joe's keys to Andy. "Open the projection window." He pops the lid off the canister and fits the reel onto the projector.

"You know how to work that thing?" Andy says.

"Demps, your sorry ass is about to be saved by the president of AV Club."

Andy makes a grunting sound that Carl thinks might have been a laugh.

As soon as Andy slides the window open, Carl flips on the projector. The boys stare at the screen off in the distance, now flickering bright and counting down from three...two...

The first shot is a wide-angle view of Janesburg. People line both sides of Main, waving and cheering as

a parade passes by. The grinning fire chief tosses candy from the cab of Engine One. Then come banner-carrying representatives of the Kiwanis Club, the Rotary Club, the VFW, the high school marching band, Future Farmers of America...

"The Janesburg Founders' Day parade," Andy says.

"Shhh." Carl is concentrating. He can tell by the clothes and hairstyles of the extras in the crowd that this movie was shot about a decade after the first, yet when the camera cuts to Sam and Stan, who watch the parade from a second-story window, they are still teenagers. They're being played by different actors now, but Stan's head is wrapped in bandages, and what can be seen of his skin is covered in fake Silly Putty scars.

Carl can also tell Jasper Reid didn't make this film. The shots are shorter, jumpier. The angles aren't as refined. *Joe,* thinks Carl, *is this your movie?*

On screen, Sam and Stan crouch below the sill of their window and watch a swarm of moths descend on Main Street. Many cheerful expressions turn to annoyance as the townspeople swat at the moths. Then their faces go slack.

What follows is a bloodbath. The infested turn on their friends, families, neighbors and choke, bludgeon, stab. The fire chief drives Engine One into a crowd of terrified bystanders, pulping some beneath his tires, crushing others against the side of the post office. Soon, the only people left standing are those controlled by parasites. Placid now, they fall in line and walk single-file down the center of the street. Wobbly close-ups show egg sacs hanging from their ears.

Back to Sam and Stan. Sam swats the side of his face and digs a finger into his ear. A close-up of Stan's horrified eyes switches to a close-up of Stan's scarred hand clutching an ice pick. *Eyes. Ice pick. Eyes. Ice pick.* An egg sac billows from Sam's ear. Stan raises the ice pick but can't bring himself to land the blow. Sam rises and calmly exits the room. From the window, Stan watches Sam walk out into the street and join the parasite parade.

"If all this happened, why doesn't anyone in town remember?" Andy whispers.

"I don't know. Maybe they meant it to be an allegory or something."

"What's an allegory?"

"A story that cuts to the point. Like you're not supposed to take it literally."

"Oh. Well, where are they going?"

Carl's pretty sure he knows. A queasy feeling turns his stomach.

On screen, Stan runs into the street. Ears bandaged, he tiptoes after the mindless townspeople, keeping his distance. Sure enough, they make their way to a giant meteor crater at the edge of town.

"Is that *this* crater?" Andy squeaks. "I mean, shit! Is that where we are right now?"

"You know a different giant crater outside Janesburg? Now shut up. This is where we learn what to do."

The townspeople stand at the crater's edge. The ground at the bottom of the crater quakes and cracks and splits apart. A giant black wing the size of a barn door unfolds from the ground. Then another. Two shiny forelegs follow, joints clicking and clacking. The queen. Slowly, she climbs from her subterranean nest, a massive moth-like alien nightmare. She shakes out hairy, black antennae, each some five or six feet long. Fully emerged, she stands as tall as the crater is deep. Rearing up on her hind legs, she uncurls a spindly proboscis. One by one, she plucks the egg sacs from the townspeople's ears and tucks them into a pouch in her abdomen. One by one, the townspeople fall dead, their purpose served.

That's how this all works, Carl realizes. He's not queasy anymore. He's fascinated. Resolute. Every ten years, the queen collects her eggs. For a decade, she incubates them. Then they hatch, and this whole cycle begins again.

The only way to break the cycle is to kill the queen.

On screen, Sam is the last to fall. Stan steps to the edge of the crater and lets out a primal scream. The queen swings her head around to face him. He's ready to do battle. He's ready to…

The ground beneath the projection shack bucks, sending Carl and Andy sprawling against the door. The projector pitches off its stand and crashes to the floor. With a crunch of breaking glass, the drive-in goes dark.

"Fuck!" Andy shouts. "She's here!"

Carl scrambles toward the projector and yanks on the reel, but it's stuck. The shack bucks again, harder this time. *No, no, no!* That film is the only way to know how to fight the queen.

"Cramer, we have to get out of here!"

"The concession stand," Carl shouts, pulling himself to his feet. "It's concrete. It's our best chance. You still have Joe's keys?"

Andy holds up the keys, then slams open the door and takes off at a sprint. Carl moves to follow, but a third tremor rocks the flimsy shack. He slides like a bowling ball into Joe's vintage film reels, which crash and clatter down around him. A rusty reel rolls across the slanted floor, unspooling a long, curling strip of ancient celluloid.

Celluloid...

"Carl!" Andy's voice is frantic and faraway.

Some shadowy corner of Carl's brain registers that this is the first time Andy Demps has ever called him Carl, not Cramer, and he knows there's something kind of significant about that, like maybe they're becoming friends, but right now a much bigger part of his brain is spinning and spinning. He has an idea.

Celluloid...concession stand...

He has more than an idea. He has a plan.

"Open the concession stand window!" Carl screams into the darkness.

Groping along the floor, he grabs an armful of vintage film reels. Six or seven of them. He hopes that's enough. He leaps out the door just as the shack heaves again, then collapses behind him like a crushed soda can.

He lands straddling a massive crack in the ground—a crack that's getting wider and longer. It's one of many cracks, he realizes, and they're all getting wider and longer, spreading out like jagged lightning from behind him, where the shack used to be.

Slowly, he turns. A black wing emerges from beneath the wreckage of the shack, an oily black membrane unfurling like the sail of some demonic hell ship.

Carl can't breathe. Can't move. Can't even remember how. She's here. The queen. Just like in the movie. No, worse than in the movie. Much, much worse.

The clicking and clacking of massive insectile joints snaps him into action. He runs. He runs faster than he's ever run before, backpack thumping against his bony shoulder blades. He leaps over cracks, anticipating the shift and tilt of the ground as it pitches beneath his feet. He's not running away from the queen. He's running *around* her, zigzagging as he goes and flinging old film out behind him like party streamers.

"What are you doing?" Andy yells from the open window of the concession stand. "Get your ass in here!"

Carl ignores him. He's almost out of film, but that's okay because he's almost made a full circuit. A second wing emerges. He slings the last of the film over his shoulder, tosses the empty reel, and sprints toward the concession stand.

Andy holds the door open for him, then slams it and locks the deadbolt. "Either you're completely crazy or that little joy-run was part of some brilliant plan."

"Brilliant plan," Carl says, chest heaving. He grabs three large soda cups and sets them upright on the counter. His eyes sweep over the candy rack on the back wall: Twizzlers, Milk Duds, Whoppers, Gobstoppers, Junior Mints (his favorite), and...

Perfect.

He snatches all the Sour Patch Kids. "Like this," he tells Andy. He dumps three whole bags into one of the cups, then mashes the candy down with his fist. He pokes a finger into the center of the sticky, sugary mass and stuffs a napkin into the hole.

Andy glances out at the queen, now using her forelegs to haul her semi-trailer-sized thorax out of the ground. "Sour Patch Kids. Napkins. Right. Whatever you say."

Carl flings open the cabinet under the soda dispenser and yanks out all the rubber tubing. The CO_2 tank tips and rolls out of the cabinet onto the top of Carl's foot, but he barely feels the pain. He selects the longest piece of tubing and tests its stretch, then eyes the aluminum tracks bracketed to either side of the window.

"What now?" says Andy.

Carl points at the jug of Wesson cooking oil next to the popcorn maker. "Soak the napkins."

Andy nods, understanding now. "Fucking righteous!" He snatches the jug, unscrews the cap, and starts tipping oil into the cups.

Carl's cheeks flush, but the queen's third set of legs is now scrabbling out onto the broken, churned-up ground, so he tells himself there'll be plenty of time to be proud later, after he kills the queen. Fingers fumbling, he knots one end of the tubing to the track, then stretches it across the window and ties off the other end. Praying, he pulls the tubing back like a bow string and lets go. The knots hold. The tubing snaps taut with a satisfying thwack.

Show time.

"We should be making, like, a hundred of these," Andy says.

Carl pulls the matchbook from his back pocket and tosses it to Andy. "Only three matches left. Let's make 'em count."

Andy lights a match and drops it into the first cup. The oily napkin ignites. A second later, the sugar-coated candy begins to burn.

Suddenly, they have the queen's full attention. Her colossal head swings toward them. The candy bomb's tiny flame is reflected a million times in her scaly black eyes.

Heart thumping, Carl pulls the cup against the tubing, aims, and releases. It hits the ground a good twenty yards short of the queen. The flame burns out in a sad little wisp of smoke.

"Jesus, Cramer!" Andy lights another match and drops it into the second cup. "What are you aiming for?"

"The celluloid." Carl squints at the shiny ribbons of film that crisscross the ground in a giant ring around the queen. He takes candy bomb number two and holds his breath. This time, he pulls the tubing back a little harder. Holding his breath, he lets go.

This one, too, falls short and burns out.

The queen's antennae swish and flick. She hunches, her clickety, clackity legs clicking and clacking. It's a defensive posture if ever Carl saw one. She's figured it out.

"The cell-you-what?"

"The old film. It's highly flammable."

"*That* was your plan?" Andy looks like he's not sure he should waste the last match, the last flaming candy bomb, on Carl's poor decisions.

"Give it to me," Carl says. "I've got the feel of it now. I'll make it count."

Maybe Andy realizes that trusting Carl has gotten him this far. Maybe he's just plain scared he couldn't do any better. Or maybe it's because Andy's a football player and respects the potential glory of a good Hail Mary. Whatever the reason, Andy crosses himself, lights the final match, and hands Carl the last candy bomb.

Carl nocks the bomb against the tubing. He stares straight into the queen's gigantic, faceted eyes. "Die, you alien parasite bitch."

He lets go.

The celluloid ring goes up in a flash, a silo of fire rising up around the queen. She rears up on her hind legs, a deafening screech tearing out of whatever orifice approximates a throat. With a mighty leap, she takes to the sky, massive wings beating wind into the hot night air.

And then she's gone.

The celluloid ring burns out nearly as fast as it went up. Once again, the night is dark and silent.

"Well," Carl says, "that didn't go quite like I hoped."

"Are you shitting me, man? She's gone! We're still alive."

Carl hears genuine admiration in Andy's voice, but this is a minor victory. "She'll be back."

"Maybe she'll build a nest somewhere else."

"Either way, we're probably the only two people in the world who know she exists. It's up to us to warn people."

"How?"

"We do what Jasper and Scar-y Joe did. We make a movie." Carl reaches into his backpack and pulls out Andy's Nebraska cap. "You in, Demps?"

Andy swallows hard. For a moment, the boys are silent, staring at the cap and thinking about a girl they both loved.

Then Andy takes his cap and pulls it onto his head. "Yeah, Cramer. I'm in."

NEGATIVE CREEP

ALVARO ZINOS-AMARO

NEGATIVE CREEP

ALVARO ZINOS-AMARO

"**C**hop chop, dickweed."

The burly orderly jostles Daniel. Daniel's stainless steel cuffs clink, and he resumes the long march down the dreary hall leading to his new residence. Patients at the Arvada Sanatorium—formerly the Colorado State Psychiatric Institute—call this infamous cell Silent Night.

Doctor Sapermann pushes a gray medication cart. Daniel closes his eyes, relishing the sound of its squeaky wheels.

Ten feet from Silent Night, he stops, falling to his knees.

"Oh, fuck this," the orderly says. Strong hands grip Daniel's underarms and yank him off the floor, dragging him the remaining distance.

A final shove slams him inside Silent Night's padded white interior.

Dr. Sapermann lifts up a clipboard from his cart and with gleeful fastidiousness makes a notation. "You don't look so hot, kid," he says.

The words remind Daniel of some movie he saw years ago, involving dream warriors. He doesn't respond. His vocal chords are shot from a night of screaming and raving. Not that much sound would get through the muzzle anyway.

"We good?" the orderly asks.

The doctor stares at Daniel. "Behave," he says, "and we'll remove the cuffs tomorrow."

Dr. Sapermann nods at the orderly, and the orderly pushes the heavy door, which begins its ponderous, inward swing.

When it enters Daniel's field of vision, the door's small, double-paned, mesh-grid window offers a refracted view of the two men, appearing now as wavering homunculi.

As the heavy door moves towards the latch, Daniel loses himself in time, surrendering to the infinitely satisfying whine of its rusty hinges, measuring out his heartbeats until—

A Week Earlier

"I don't think it was murder," Jared said, lowering his gaze. "Dawn never hurt a soul, and they didn't even take her wallet."

The four of them sat in Daniel's beat-up Buick Skyhawk, barely glancing at the images projected on the huge movie screen five car rows ahead. Daniel couldn't remember a time when gathering at the 88 Drive-In had ever been somber, until today.

"… *welcome to Ludlow,*" a tinny voice said on the car

stereo. "*Hope your time here will be a happy one.*" His speech was punctuated by a beat of silence and then the heavy roar of a rumbling long-haul truck. Daniel dialed down the sound.

Rhonda fidgeted in the seat behind Jared. "Maybe—I mean, she had been fighting with her mom—maybe... Dawn took her own life," she said.

"How dare you?" Daniel asked, biting off each word.

"Easy," Tara said from the seat behind Daniel's. "We're just trying to figure this thing out, Danny boy. We're all on edge, okay? So cut us some slack." Her voice went up. "Am I the only one who's been hearing weird sounds recently?"

"Oh shit," Jared said.

"Kinda like static, but denser somehow," Rhonda said. "It's happened to me twice."

"A hum that gets louder and louder," Tara said. "A... voice underneath."

"Stop it," Daniel said. "This is not the time to be losing our goddamn minds. Didn't you just come back from a weekend in the mountains, Tara? So maybe it was your ears popping."

"And me?" Rhonda said.

"Your headaches," Daniel muttered. "Migraines can do that."

"Jesus Christ, I did not imagine I heard—"

"I heard it too," Jared interrupted. "Whatever got to Dawn could be coming after us next."

Tara leaned forward. "What makes you say that, Jared?"

In the rearview mirror Daniel studied Tara's expression. Her dark brown eyes had a melancholy cast, and her long black hair seemed to have lost its usual luster. But she was still in control. That made him angry.

"My sister and Dawn were like best friends, and she gave me something," Jared said. "I dunno, I guess she just didn't want the cops to have it."

"Well, what is it?" Tara asked.

Daniel's fingers wrapped themselves around the Buick's steering wheel. "You've had something from Dawn this whole time and you're only telling us now?"

"That's not fair," Tara chided.

"It's only been three days," Jared said, looking away.

Daniel swallowed. He forced his hands to ease up, color slowly filling in his knuckle whites. "Feels like a hell of a lot longer," he said.

Rhonda reached forward and placed her hand on Jared's shoulder. "Did you bring it with you?"

Jared grabbed his schoolbag and pulled out a small violet box. It had Dawn's name written on the lid's flower-shaped sticker. With exaggerated reverence, Jared opened the box and pulled out a notebook. "My sister found it in Dawn's room when she searched for her that night. Sort of a diary," he said. Shame tinged his cheeks magenta. "I just skimmed it."

Rhonda said, "Maybe there's something in there about her family…"

Daniel turned in his seat. "For the last time," he said, "she didn't fucking kill herself. Dawn's issues with her mom were nothing like yours with your dad."

Rhonda flinched and then averted her gaze. "Jerk," she mumbled.

Tara fixed her eyes squarely on the notebook. "May I?"

Jared passed it to her.

Tara flipped through its pages, eyes roving hungrily.

Daniel waited for something, for anything, to happen, waited for his life to go back to how it had been, knowing it never would. Up on the theater screen, a man picked up a cat and an Orinco tanker rushed by.

"Guys, I think there may be some clues in here," Tara said a minute later. "Dawn says she thought there might be someone... or some*thing*... stalking her. She talks about her hippie parents having been involved with some weird New Age group in Manitou Springs. She suspected they performed a ritual, and something went wrong. A force was unleashed. And—"

"Let me see that," Daniel snapped, snatching the diary.

After a few seconds he realized its scrawl was a struggle to decipher. Embarrassed, he closed it. "Go on."

"Like I was saying," Tara continued, unfazed, "Dawn believed that this group her parents fell in with tapped into some kind of energy from another realm, and once it crossed over to our world, it was somehow drawn to movies—a kind of electromagnetic resonance. That's why she went to the Landmark that night. She was trying to steal film reels, to perform an experiment."

Jared frowned. "That sounds pretty far out," he said. "Maybe Dawn was, uh, troubled in ways we didn't know about."

"You know what, Jared?" Daniel said, face twisted into a grimace. "It takes a schizo to know one."

Jared drew back. His face fell and he blinked back tears.

"Shit, Danny, give it up already!" Tara said.

Daniel heaved a massive breath and counted off seconds. Then he said, "Look man, I'm sorry. I didn't mean it, okay?"

But the truth was that a part of him *had* meant it. Daniel hadn't wanted to believe the rumors that started up during the second semester of junior high, but when Jared returned to school, after his parents pulled him out for over a month, he had to admit he saw his friend in a different light.

It took a few moments for Jared to accept the peace offering. When they shook hands Daniel noticed Jared's clamminess and withdrew a little too quickly.

"Better," Tara said. "Look, Danny. We know you had a thing for Dawn. I get it—it's hard. But she was our friend too. Try to keep that in mind."

Fuck you, thought Daniel, but held quiet. There was nothing to say. Tara would never understand the depth of his feelings for Dawn, and the regret he'd have to live with the rest of his life for having been too much of a

coward to act on them. Maybe if he'd been braver, things would have played out differently. Heck, Dawn might still be alive today.

The conversation continued, but Daniel was no longer listening. He felt mummified by grief. With tremendous effort, he pierced the gauze of numbness, and tried again to read the diary. This time the letters came together. On the last few pages he noticed a recurring symbol he'd missed the first time: − | ✜ | −.

He lifted up the diary and pointed at the symbol. "Did you see this?"

"Yes," Tara said. "No idea what it means."

"So we agree," Rhonda said, continuing the exchange Daniel zoned out on. "Until we know more, *we stay away from movies and TV.*"

"It can't hurt," Jared said.

"Right," Tara said. "Daniel?"

He swallowed. "Sure, whatever. But the diary stays with me."

Jared was on the cusp of speaking, but Tara intervened. "Fine," she said. "It's yours for twenty-four hours. And then it goes back to Jared, so he can return it to his sister."

Daniel looked at the movie screen. Characters were wandering through a macabre graveyard. He changed the radio to a rock station. "Let's get the hell out of here," he said, and started up the engine.

"I've got it," Tara yelled, picking up the upstairs receiver before her brother had the chance to interfere.

"It's me," Daniel said. He sounded distant.

"I had a feeling you were going to call," Tara whispered.

A pause. "You did?"

"I can't explain it. I've been thinking about the diary ever since you dropped us off at Tony's Diner. Something about that symbol."

"Yeah," Daniel said. "It gets under your skin."

Tara visualized it now: − | ✤ | −. It danced on her retinas. Entranced, she said nothing.

"Actually, that's what I'm calling about," Daniel said. "I think I've figured it out, or part of it. Dawn was onto something. But I think she had it backwards. The thing does react to films, but it isn't drawn to them—it's repelled by them."

As though on cue, sounds from the trashy movie Tara's brother was watching in the living room drifted up the staircase. It hadn't exactly been difficult for Tara to turn him down for *Sleepaway Camp III: Teenage Wasteland*, the latest tape he'd borrowed from Daniel. And now, to think that if Daniel was right, she might have to watch it herself, and actually do the babysitting she'd promised her parents—outrageous. "... *let's all sing a rousing camp song*," a film voice said. "*Does anyone know 'I'm a Happy Camper'*?"

Tara said, "What did Dawn want with the film reels?"

"That part's confusing," Daniel said. "But I think she was trying to figure out if messing around with film—playing it in reverse, projecting a negative, whatever—would have any effect on the entity." His voice became hushed. "You were right, Tara. Dawn wrote about a sound only she could hear. She wondered if she was losing her marbles or it was something more."

"So what makes you think movies ward this thing off?"

"Dawn used the symbol more often when she was alone, in silence," Daniel said. "When she watched something, the entity wasn't around."

Tara straightened a strand of hair. "Maybe it's not just movies then," she said. "Maybe it's *any* kind of sound or noise."

"Hmmm." Daniel's breathing quickened. The words tumbled out of him. "That could fit. When she was killed in the theater, it was dark, quiet. She was alone. And the projection booth is soundproofed. Can you tell Jared and Rhonda right away? They need to have sound around them at all times."

When Tara left Tony's she'd gotten the impression that Rhonda was enjoying Jared's company and wasn't eager to go home. With luck they'd still be at the diner. She'd grab some of the VHS tapes her brother borrowed from Daniel to give to Rhonda and Jared as ammunition and listen to her Walkman on the way. "Okay," she said. "What're you gonna do?"

"I'm going to test our theory," he said.

It isn't fair, Jared thought as he stepped into the shower, radio blaring from the sink-adjacent shelf. As the hot water sprayed against his blonde hair and fair skin, he wondered for the umpteenth time if the torture inside his head would ever let up. For awhile, after the therapy his parents arranged for him, he'd been doing better. He'd felt in control of his desires. But recently his instincts reasserted themselves, seemingly stronger than ever, and his inner defenses were crumbling. Was thinking about boys really a sin? Didn't everyone fantasize one way or another?

And now, he thought as he grabbed the soap and lathered himself, everything was even *more* messed up.

He'd suspected for a while that Daniel was into Dawn, but hearing it from Tara today finally made it real. God, what a fool he'd been to think that he and Daniel could ever share something special. Not only that, but Rhonda started sending Jared signals, subtle when the four of them had been in the car, unmistakable when it was just them at the diner. He'd have to make excuses to—

"*He walks on, doesn't look back,*" the voice on the radio sang, seemingly tapping into his thoughts, "*he pretends he can't hear her.*"

He was so sick of that new single; they were playing it to death.

Without warning, he heard the door to the bathroom open. "Jared, I told you, you can't use my radio in here!" his sister harrumphed. A second later the door closed, and she and the music were gone.

Tara's warning rang loudly in Jared's mind: *No matter what, keep some kind of sound on around you at all times. Promise me.* He'd tried watching the tapes Tara had given him, apparently part of Daniel's collection, but had soon discovered that they weren't his speed. He'd only made it fifteen minutes into *Student Bodies*, less than ten into *Graduation Day*, and he'd barely endured the main title sequence of *Splatter University* before deciding he needed to cleanse himself with a shower.

At least the water jet was pretty loud. Just to be safe, he made it stronger, and hotter.

His body flushed at the surge. Surprisingly, his frustration began to melt away. He was going to stop trying to live up to what others expected from him and just be himself, he decided. The enormous pressure he'd been carrying in his neck and temples for days now lightened. Lathering up some more, he let his hands dwell on his groin. Was it such a bad thing? How he'd missed it. He longed for it. The relief; the feeling of being whole, alive. He started stroking himself. The soft pleasurable moan that followed was buried under the showerhead's steady jet.

His hand moved with increasing speed. God, he was seconds away from release. It had been too long. He closed his eyes and slowed down in anticipation.

The showerhead sputtered.

Droplets dribbled, then nothing.

Just my luck, Jared thought. The old showerhead must have gotten clogged.

He was so close. Screw it. He started again.

That was when he heard it—no, *felt* it. Not a sound anywhere specific but somehow everywhere at once. An enveloping curtain, a change in the air pressure. He opened his eyes, became immediately flaccid. "Mom?" he called out, his voice feeling tiny. "Is that you?"

Keep it together, he told himself. He tried banging on the showerhead. It rattled and hiccupped a small flurry of water, but that was it. Shivering, he grabbed his towel and stepped out of the shower, trying to think of something to sing. That was when the charge, the presence, returned.

It was stronger this time, a palpable force with a distinct pitch and vibration. The sound coalesced into an energy that seemed to seep into his skin and rummage through his insides. Riding the whirlwind were countless voices, memories, untold histories. One of the voices rose above the others. "A BATH WILL MAKE ME FEEL BETTER," –|✤|– blasted. "WILL YOU WAIT WITH HER WHILE I CLEAN UP?"

"Mom?" Jared cried out again, knowing full well it wasn't his mom, but he could no longer hear himself.

The wall of noise was all-encompassing now, simultaneously outside and inside him.

"EACH OF YOU WERE SELECTED BECAUSE YOU HAVE THIS MARK ON YOUR ARM," –|♣|– pronounced. Every syllable hammered at Jared's brain.

"What the fuck!" he croaked. "Leave me alone!"

His arms shot up and down, casting loose the towel, trying to fend off his foe but finding nothing to strike.

"ONE OF YOU IS A WEREWOLF," –|♣|– boomed.

Somewhere beyond the turbulence of his panic and a sense of unshakeable doom, Jared's mind flashed a glimmer of recognition. Those words sounded familiar. Where had he heard them before? Wasn't it… a movie? A recent flick about werewolves? Yes. They'd watched it at Daniel's place. He remembered now. *Howling V: The Rebirth*. But why would—

–|♣|– returned, inescapable, drowning out the world, obliterating everything Jared had ever known.

Rhonda fidgeted in her room, trying to find distraction in the VHS's Tara forced on her at the diner. Girl, what dreck. As much as she appreciated Tara's practical thinking, couldn't she have found something better for her than *Bloody Birthday*, *Mother's Day*, and *Happy Birthday to Me*? She wondered if Jared was having better luck with his titles. They were also from Daniel's collection, so probably not. Still, she found herself picturing Jared lying down on the couch, head tilted dreamily, smiling that lopsided smile of his that dimpled his cheeks, his blue eyes—

Stop it Rhonda, she told herself. The whole point of watching this crap—besides, if Daniel and Tara's theory was correct, the small business of survival—was to keep her mind *off* Jared. It was clear from his behavior at the diner that he wasn't interested.

She sighed. Enough of this. She needed to clear her head. Remembering her promise to Tara, she started up her Discman and put on her headphones. Janet Jackson's peppy *Rhythm Nation 1814* lifted her mood. Remembering that her Discman had been skipping lately, she tucked her Walkman into one of her overalls pockets as a backup.

Knowing her dad would disapprove of a solo expedition after sunset, she snuck out through the garage.

She walked fast in the cool evening air. How silly, she thought, to have gotten worked up over Jared. There was so much more to life. Her crush would pass. Just then "*Miss You Much*" piped through her headphones, and she rolled her eyes at fate's irony.

Two songs later, she noticed the Discman was warm in her hand. Damn, she thought, here we go. Sure enough, it started skipping. She stopped, pulled out her Walkman, and smoothly transferred the headphones over.

She pushed the Walkman's "Play" button.

Nothing happened.

"What the hell?" she said.

She took out the tape, spooled it with her pinkie to make sure it was working, and re-inserted it.

The air seemed to have grown colder.

Come on, come on, she thought, and hit "Play" again, hard.

Still no dice.

Then a scythe of sound felled the silence around her. The fleeting blow with a presence that shouldn't have been there sent her tumbling back.

Nerves frayed, she launched into an off-key rendition of a childhood lullaby. Then she decided to check the Walkman's battery compartment, because, even though she'd put new batteries in only three days before, what the heck else could it be?

Behind the little plastic cover, she found a paper strip and no batteries. Irritatingly familiar print spelled out a message on the paper strip: "We talked about you listening to this kind of stuff. Let this be a lesson. Love, Dad."

You have to be fucking kidding me, Rhonda thought. So her dad snooped through her stuff again, and her tape hadn't met with his "moral standards". In fact, the tape was a gift from Dawn, from her visit to Europe, where she'd been lucky enough to attend the Fantafestival in Rome; there she'd illicitly recorded an hour's worth of the soundtrack to the cult movie *Tetsuo: The*

Iron Giant. Rhonda chose the tape specifically because the movie's audio was an insane, impenetrable wall of noise, the perfect shield. And now her dad ruined everything.

She screamed.

And then thought: I just have to keep wailing while I run home.

She turned in the direction of her house and sprinted. Keeping up her holler while running at top speed, though, was tough. Catching her breath for a moment, she felt it again, a bubble around her, sucking out ordinary silence, replacing it with a grotesque, distorted version of itself that somehow clamored inside her mind.

It was so concussive and all-pervasive she could hardly hear her own thoughts.

"GET ON THE SNAKE WHERE THE WATER TURNS TO STEAM," − | ✤ | − howled. "GET ON THE SNAKE WITH A SUICIDE MACHINE."

She yelled at the top of her lungs, expecting to pierce her own ears with the shrill, rending cry, but she heard only a faint, muffled echo. Screeching again, she ran and ran and ran until an invisible something thrust out before her right foot, sending her tumbling down head-first on the sidewalk.

As she fell her left arm shot out in an attempt to soften the fall. Her body slammed onto the ground and her left wrist snapped from the blow, firing a lightning pulse of pain through her body. She was momentarily blinded as the right side of her face ate the pavement.

Dizzy, pain ricocheting in every fiber of her being, she moaned and twisted onto her side.

Her brain told her mouth to move, but only a sickening gurgle arose.

A crushing, soundless boom locked the world in its sonic shackles.

"THE SHEAVES HAVE ALL BEEN BROUGHT," − | ✤ | − bellowed, "BUT THE FIELDS HAVE WASHED AWAY."

Rhonda felt the walls of sound closing in, excavating out the air and universe all around her, compressing her from all sides until there was nowhere left to go.

"Consider it a work in progress," Tara said.

Daniel rubbed his hands for warmth. Despite blasting the radio in his Skyhawk during the midnight drive to this abandoned barn, every little noise on the way spooked him. At least now the film playing on the barn wall that Tara rigged into a projection area provided a steady stream of sound. But thinking about everything that had happened over the last week still chilled his core.

Half-interestedly, he examined the pile of tapes near the projector, titles like *Night of the Comet*, *Street Trash*, *The Stuff*, and *Of Unknown Origin*, all of which he'd loaned to Tara's younger brother, and which Tara had been nice enough to haul out here. Daniel brought a couple of boxes himself, but they were still in the car. His gaze wandered to the flickering movie image. "*I don't think we need to break up a family, do we Pumpkin*?" said a creepy-looking dude.

Daniel couldn't help but think about his own sundered tribe. First Dawn. Now, Jared and Rhonda. His brain couldn't handle it. Even worse, he knew the cops would want to speak to him and Tara soon.

"If we really want to make this place a safe haven," Daniel said, "and play movies twenty-four seven, we're going to need help."

"Agreed," Tara said.

She glanced back at the barn entrance.

Guess I'm not the only one who's nervous, Daniel thought. "We need to get to the bottom of whatever this creature wants," he said. "Otherwise we're just delaying the inevitable." The experiment in his closet had nearly cost him his life. He suppressed a tremor as he remembered his encounter with −|✙|−. "I let it get close to me, Tara, and I wrote down what it said. It seems to be parroting back whatever it hears. Films, songs. What I don't get is why."

Tara regarded him with eyes on the brink of an abyss. "Danny, do you ever feel like our lives are heading down the wrong path somehow?"

Daniel frowned. "Meaning?"

"Like... we're getting lost. Before we started high school, life was so simple. But now we have Walkmans

and CD players, personal computers, camcorders, Nintendo. My dad even has a car phone."

"What's wrong with that?"

A shadow flitted over Tara's face. Daniel blinked and it was gone. "What if," she said, "we've reached some kind of critical mass of distraction, and we need to be reminded to pay attention?"

Daniel bit his lower lip. "What does mirroring back sound fragments," he said, impatience swelling within, "have to do with paying attention?"

For a split second, Tara thought she heard −| ✤ |−. This time it wasn't like at the mountains, or the other times since. She held herself very still. "I think it wants us to *listen*," she said. "It wants us to understand that if we never spend time alone with our thoughts, we'll eventually go insane and die."

Again, Daniel noticed her look back at the barn entrance.

At that moment, the movie playing on the barn wall—*The Stepfather*, Daniel remembered—kicked into high gear, with the sound of a police siren gradually intruding on the scene and drowning out the dialogue.

Except, Daniel thought as he watched the scene, there was no cop car in the frame.

A moment later a voice blasted through a megaphone and the barn door burst open.

"Daniel Escalante," a police officer barked, gun drawn, "you're under arrest on suspicion of the murders of Dawn Hayes, Jared Cruz and Rhonda Watkins."

"What?! No, I—" Shaking, he turned to Tara. "You set me up, didn't you? You planned this whole thing. You—"

They cuffed him. "Son, don't make this any harder than it has to be. We don't know how you did it, but each of the victims had VHS tapes with your fingerprints on them. You're coming with us."

"How could you, Tara?" Daniel yelled as they escorted him out. "You made some kind of deal with it, didn't you?" he ranted.

Tara shook her head sadly and reached out for a hug, which the nearest officer was happy to supply. "It's so awful," she said, sobbing. "He used to be a good guy. I think maybe he watched too many of those sick movies."

She pointed to the stack of tapes near the projector, and felt a shiver of pleasure.

Now

—the door at last finishes its ponderous arc and clicks shut. From inside his cell, Daniel hears Dr. Sapermann secure the three bolt locks, sees him smirk an officious grin, and disappear into the murk beyond.

Despite his muzzle, Daniel tries to scream, but his sore vocal cords produce only a hoarse, raspy whimper.

He clinks his handcuffs together, until they begin to slice into his skin.

Then he takes a step back and jumps against the cell's padded wall, bouncing off and landing on the padded

floor with a dull thud. He stands up and does it again. And again. And again. He goes on and on until he's panting for air.

Lying on the ground now, he feels completely drained, too tired to even sit.

Finally, Daniel blinks.

He blinks as many times as he can, focusing on the almost inaudible sound of his batting eyelashes.

In time his eyelids sting and burn so that he can blink no longer.

He closes his eyes.

At last he accepts his new world of complete and utter silence.

It doesn't take long.

The voice slashes right through him. "THIS IS GETTING TO BE," drones – | ✦ | –.

HELLULOID

DAYTON WARD AND KEVIN DILMORE

HELLULOID

DAYTON WARD AND KEVIN DILMORE

A ***ugust 16, 1985***
5:30 P.M. Eastern Standard Time
"Tenebris copias, exaudi me!"

Watching the black-cloaked figure sitting cross-legged in front of him, Mitch heard mumbling he couldn't understand. He leaned closer but was still unable to make it out.

"Is that supposed to be Latin?"

The whispered question came from Mitch's right, and he turned to shush Evan, his friend and classmate.

"Quiet, man," he said, keeping his voice low.

In the light cast by candles, Mitch scanned the faces of the others seated with him around a wobbly-lined pentagram drawn in white chalk on the concrete floor. To the cloaked figure's right was Kate, a senior and the oldest of the bunch. She offered Mitch a smirk and brushed back her brown bangs to better focus on the ritual. Trey sat next to her, smiling as if he had just staged the stunt of the century. Mitch shook his head.

I can't believe we're doing this.

From under the dark figure's hood came a low-pitched but clearly feminine voice, this time with words Mitch understood. "Wreakers of vengeance and spite, Arcana summons you to our bidding."

"No way," Evan interrupted again. "Sandy?"

The girl's voice did not waver. "You shall address me as Arcana."

"Horse shit, *Sandy.*" Evan's laughter filled the darkened room. "I should've known." He sneered at Trey. "Your girlfriend's a fucking witch?"

"I prefer 'necromancer', Evan," replied Sandy, her tone one of loathing as she confirmed to Mitch that Evan was correct. "And could you maybe not be such a dick?"

Trey scowled at Evan. "Yeah, quit being a dick, Evan." The senior sounded confrontational, but Mitch knew Trey was no tough guy—especially not with the Andrew McCarthy haircut he sported.

"Can we just do this and get back to work? Please? We need to get ready for showtime." Mitch was getting the feeling this whole thing was a really bad idea.

He hated coming down on his friends like this, but he was still their boss. In the spring, Mitch had been promoted to acting manager of his shifts at the Vogue Theater. It was a role he did his best to take seriously despite his staff all being kids he knew from school, and most of them a year older. However, given the circumstances, he welcomed anything that boosted morale—even a half-assed arcane ritual in the theater's basement. While it might not keep the Vogue from closing, maybe it would give the owner, old man Cowen, a demonic case of the shits.

Wicked shits, Mitch mused. *And no toilet paper.*

"We demand your service," said Sandy, returning to her deep Arcana voice. Mitch watched her right hand disappear beneath the cloak between her legs and emerge grasping a plastic cup of blueberry yogurt. "Strike down our foe, Mr. Cowen, before he wrongs us!"

"Sandy, wait," Mitch blurted as she brought her other hand to the yogurt cup and tore off its plastic lid.

"*Lavetur in nobis sanguis tyrranus!*"

She spilled the cup's contents into the center of the pentagram. Instead of yogurt, a dark red liquid struck the floor, spattering everyone sitting in the circle.

Kate yelped. "Gross! What are you doing?"

Before Mitch could say anything else, a hard thump shook the floor, coursing up and through his body. A sound like shattering glass rang in his ears, and for a moment he lost his breath like the time he stood too close to a mortar firing at the town's annual Fourth of July show. Was it an earthquake? Had a car jumped the curb and hit the theater? Evan sprang to his feet and looked around as though preparing to bolt up the basement steps.

"What the hell was that?"

Adjusting the hood of her cloak, Sandy blew out the candles. "The forces of retribution have been unleashed."

"Sure. Okay." Kate cast a disbelieving look at Mitch.

"Should we call old man Cowen and see if he's been exorcised or teleported to Hell or whatever?"

Trey helped Mitch to his feet and then clapped a hand on the shoulder of Mitch's red blazer.

"Pretty cool, huh?"

"Whatever." As he brushed dust off the seat of his new khaki pants, Mitch shifted to what Evan called his boss voice. "Let's get ready to open. Trey, go see if anything happened upstairs."

He watched Evan lead Trey and Sandy out of the basement before a glint of light flashed in the corner of his eye. Turning in that direction, Mitch saw a framed picture, which normally hung above the desk belonging to the theater's custodian, Oliver LeWayne, laying on the floor, its glass cracked in several places. Cursing under his breath, Mitch walked over to the broken picture and plucked it up. He grimaced as he studied the autographed photo of a beautiful, raven-haired woman. The handwriting was as exquisite as the face in the picture.

To Oliver. All my best, Bettina Ortiz.

"Who is she?" Kate asked.

"Dunno." Mitch laid the broken memento on the desk. "Movie star from the 50s, I think. I bet LeWayne's had it hanging there for years."

Kate eyed the photo. "Guess you shouldn't have invited a witch to the theater."

"That was *not* my idea—"

His words caught in his throat as Kate rested her hand on his wrist. "Relax. Trey already took all the credit. It was a fun diversion, if nothing else. Blow it off."

"I just...well, the whole thing kinda sucks." Mitch's eyes dropped to Kate's hand. Since Mr. Cowen announced he was closing the Vogue, he knew it was only a matter of days until he would be back to exchanging awkward hellos with Kate in the halls at school.

"Got another job lined up yet?" she asked. "I'm going to work at my uncle's greenhouse, and I can put in a good word for you. It'd be fun."

Mitch hadn't considered that possibility. "You wanna have fun? With *me?*"

Kate reached up to tug on his clip-on bow tie, which prompted a laugh from each of them. She gestured toward the pentagram and the mess left behind by Sandy. "We should take care of this before LeWayne gets back. Let's get this place open, and then I'll help you clean up down here."

"Well," Mitch said. "That certainly sounds like...*fun.*"

She slapped his arm, laughing at him before he led her out of the basement, hitting the light switch on their way out.

Only the feeble illumination from the desk's lamp saved the basement from total darkness. Then, the lamp shifted its position so its beam shone on the floor, highlighting the pentagram and the dark red liquid discoloring and dissolving its chalk outline. No sooner did light fall across the crude drawing than several puddles of the fluid quivered, rippling as they rose from the dirty concrete floor.

They drifted across the room, blending into four distinct shapes which bent and folded until they touched the middle of the basement's far wall. The shapes collided with the dingy, old plaster, flattening and stretching until they formed a set of letters spelling out a single word.

HERE.

Music blared in the projection booth, but Evan was oblivious to it. Hunched over the editing table, he gripped a box cutter and touched its razor-sharp blade to the far edge of a 35mm film strip before him. Each time he cut the film, his hand shook as his thoughts returned to the basement.

What the hell was that all about? Had Trey's girl-friend really summoned a spirit or demon or some other damned thing? He didn't want to believe such silliness, but something had happened down there.

It's Trey, Evan decided. *He and his girlfriend were screwing with us. Had to be.*

Confident he solved the mystery, he pressed the box cutter's blade between a pair of the film's sprocket holes and made his first successful slice.

"*Fuck* yeah!" Evan didn't need to shout each time he made an edit, but he did it anyway. To him, shouting swear words was a perk of working in the soundproof

projection booth. Another was cranking up his music loud enough for the beat of the Thompson Twins to shake the metal film reels in their shipping cases. What he didn't expect to hear was the heavy crash of a projection reel dropping the first hour of the night's movie to the booth's linoleum floor.

"Shit!"

Evan lunged for the projector. The reel's fall ripped the film from the gears through which it had been threaded. People would be buying tickets and entering the theater before long, and now he was nowhere near ready. "Shit, shit, shit!"

He heard film stock spilling from his editing table onto the floor, as though someone had pulled it away. Celluloid from the reel in Evan's hands began snaking around his arms and wrists, tightening by unseen forces. More of the film wrapped around his legs and bound his arms to his sides.

"What the fuck?"

Anything else Evan might have said was lost as the table's remaining contents flew at him: metal reels, tools, his paper cup of Dr Pepper. He grunted in pain under the assault of the impacts striking his chest. The force toppled him, and he landed hard on the floor. Squirming in mounting terror, Evan struggled to free himself from the strands of film doing their damnedest to mummify him…

Mitch turned from where he swabbed at the kettle of the theater's trusty, decades-old popcorn machine, looking to where Kate stood inside the small vestibule that was the Vogue's box office. Not much bigger than a closet, she had raised the curtains covering the curved front window facing the street, and the cash and ticket drawers were open as she inventoried their contents.

"Seen Trey?" he asked. "Maybe we should make him clean the basement."

Grabbing bills from the cash drawer, Kate frowned and nodded back over her shoulder. "I think he's in the stockroom. You know, with *Arcana.*"

I should've known.

Trey and Sandy had been an item all summer, practically fused at the hip. She was a frequent visitor to the Vogue when he was working, and Mitch cautioned him more than once about not letting her interfere with his responsibilities. With rare exceptions, Trey tended to heed such warnings.

Tonight was looking like one of those exceptions.

Swinging the kettle up until its drive shaft clicked into place, Mitch grunted in irritation. "Now I *know* he's cleaning the basement, and maybe the bathrooms, too."

He rounded the countertop and started across the lobby just as the stockroom door burst open and Trey and Sandy spilled out onto the carpet. They were an oily tangle of arms, legs, and partially undone clothing.

"Holy shit!"

Inside the stockroom, cases of candy and bags of uncooked popcorn cascaded from shelves onto the floor. All of it mixed with the contents of a fifty-pound pail of cooking oil that seemed to have exploded everywhere, coating everything including the decidedly unhappy couple.

"What did you do?" shouted Mitch.

Pulling himself to his feet as he tugged one arm through the sleeve of his uniform shirt, Trey waved toward the stockroom. "We didn't do anything!"

"Everything just started flying around by itself," said Sandy, her expression taut as she pulled her robe tight around her.

A loud, metallic bang echoed in the lobby and Mitch turned to see Kate scampering from the box office. Behind her, tickets, money, and other papers swirled inside the vestibule before its door slammed shut.

"What the hell is going on?" she cried, sprinting to join the others.

Trey said, "It's like the whole place is losing its mind."

"Where's Evan?" asked Kate.

The question gave Mitch a sudden chill. "Up in the booth." He looked toward the stairwell door leading to the Vogue's projection booth. "We should check on him." As if on cue, the stairwell door flung open and Evan spilled into the lobby. Strips of film wrapped around his torso and hung from his arms and legs. Mitch and Trey froze in their tracks as Kate shrieked at the sight. Even Sandy muttered something in surprise that Mitch couldn't make out. For an insane moment he wondered if she was offering more Latin.

Stumbling to his knees, Evan scrambled to regain his feet while pulling at the celluloid clinging to him. "Look out! Everybody get back!"

His warning was not fast enough, as Mitch saw a pair of metal film reels blast from the stairwell, trailing strips of film that moved like tentacles. One of the reels smacked Trey across his forehead, knocking him to the floor. Mitch managed to duck the other but could not avoid the tangles of film fluttering in its wake. A warbled whistling filled the lobby as the strips latched onto him, wrapping around his arms and legs. He felt slices of pain from the film's edges slashing his face and hands.

Sandy screamed and bolted behind the concession stand, and Mitch felt the film loosen its hold. He thought it might go after Sandy, but the strands instead pulled together, forming a swirling mass of celluloid with ends clutching the pair of film reels. The whistle intensified to a horrific roar before the mass shot across the lobby and vanished through the door leading into the auditorium.

"Holy shit!" cried Kate. Running to Mitch, she knelt beside him and put her hand on his shoulder.

Sitting on the floor and holding a hand to his bleeding forehead, Trey looked at Mitch and Kate. His face

was a mask of disbelief.

"No. Fucking. Way."

Mitch squeezed Kate's arm before turning to Evan, who was tugging film strips from his body. "Are you okay?"

His eyes wide with terror, Evan yanked the last of the film stock from around his wrists and threw it on the carpet.

"Dude, I am most certainly *not* okay!"

Elbowing his way past Mitch and Kate, he sprinted for the door leading to the street. He pushed through it, narrowly avoiding Oliver LeWayne, the Vogue's custodian.

"What the hell?" LeWayne shouted, surprised at the near miss. Mitch watched him glare at Evan as the boy ran from the theater.

Mumbling something under his breath, LeWayne made his way into the lobby. He wore a bright yellow tank top and blue Spandex shorts. A pair of white tennis shoes completed the ensemble, as bright as the sweatband he wore on his balding head. Mitch knew LeWayne had recently started attending classes at the Jazzercise studio across the street. He hoped never to see the older man dressed for the occasion.

"What are you kids standing around here for?" he asked. "Don't we have a movie to show?"

Before Mitch could answer, the concession stand's showcase windows shattered. Sandy screamed as glass and candy peppered the lobby carpet. Behind Kate, the popcorn maker spewed kernels in all directions.

"Look out!" LeWayne shouted, waving his arms as he rushed toward Mitch and the others. "Move!"

Mitch heard the cracking of wood and plaster from somewhere above him. Looking up, he saw the Vogue's signature lobby chandelier along with a sizable chunk of art deco ceiling giving way. All of it plummeted to the carpet behind LeWayne as he hustled them toward the auditorium.

Mitch was first through the door. Stepping into the theater, he noted numerous seats tossed in every direction after apparently being ripped from the floor. At least a dozen lay on the stage in front of the large screen, which bore several tears in its thick fabric.

Entering the theater behind Kate, Sandy, and Trey, LeWayne pulled the door shut. "Okay, guys," he said, trying to catch his breath. "What did Evan do now?"

"It wasn't him," Mitch replied. "We were in the basement, and Trey's girlfriend had us do this weird-assed séance. She's some kind of witch or something."

LeWayne's gaze shifted between Mitch and Sandy. "You brought a witch in here? Are you out of your damned minds?"

"Necromancer," Sandy snapped, rolling her eyes.

Mitch held up his hands. "Wasn't my idea. Talk to Trey."

"It was just a goof!" Trey said, looking to Sandy. "I don't even believe in this witch stuff."

Sandy snarled at him. "Necromancer!"

"What the fuck *ever*, Sandy!" Kate looked to LeWayne. "We never thought something like this would happen."

"Maybe not anywhere else," LeWayne countered. "But the Vogue is different. It's haunted, has been for years, and I think your witch-friend here just pissed it off."

Trey rolled his eyes. "Haunted? Now he tells us."

"Uh, guys?"

It was Sandy, pointing toward the front of the theater. Mitch turned and his eyes widened at the sight of the mass hovering above the first row of seats. The huge knot of film was as large as a person, tendrils of celluloid flapping and twisting outward from the core of the shape's bulk. Film reels hung from the ends of various strands.

Mitch jumped when a beam of light shot toward the screen from behind him, realizing it was the projector upstairs coming to life.

"Who's up there?" asked Kate.

Next to her, Trey replied, "Nobody."

"Somebody," countered Sandy. She pointed to the screen. "Look."

The beam passed through the film mass, but rather than casting a shadow, Mitch saw a portrait he recognized being projected onto the theater screen.

"Wait," Kate said. "Is that…?"

Mitch nodded. "The woman in the picture over LeWayne's desk."

"What?" asked Trey. "You roused a fucking ghost? For real? Did you say the spell backwards or something?"

Sandy scowled. "It wasn't a spell. Damn."

"Bettina?" shouted LeWayne, holding up his hands as he stepped toward the screen. "It has to be."

Mitch moved to stand beside him. "Bettina Ortiz. She was in movies, wasn't she?"

LeWayne answered with a nod, his eyes not leaving the screen. "Back in the 1950s when this place was new, you know, like Veronica Lake or Rita Hayworth. We hosted a premiere for her new big movie, and she took a liking to the owner at the time, Jack Martel."

As though reacting to the name, the mass of film twisted and whipped several of the reels in the air above itself. On the screen, the image of Bettina Ortiz stretched and contracted.

"Don't rile it, man," cautioned Trey.

Stepping closer, Kate asked, "What happened to her?"

"Back then I was an usher, and I saw them during the movie," LeWayne replied. "They couldn't keep their hands off each other, and they went out after it was over." He turned to face the group. "That was the last time anyone saw her. Martel told the cops she'd had it with the pressure of being a star. She wanted out, and decided to disappear and start a new life somewhere else. Cops grilled him for days, but they never found any evidence, and he stuck to his story.

He seemed pretty shook up, but I was sure he'd done something. The case went cold. He ended up dying a few years later. Guess he slipped while he was down in the basement and cracked his head on the concrete." Mitch asked, "And you think this place is haunted because of her?"

"I always knew something was off, especially when I became the custodian. All kinds of weird things, late at night when I was alone. Nothing bad, but I sometimes got the feeling someone was there in the basement with me." LeWayne shook his head. "All this time, it was her."

"She was trying to communicate," said Sandy. "For some reason, she was reaching out to you."

Clattering film reels made everyone jump, and Mitch saw the mass uncoiling as various strands headed for the door in the theater's far corner.

"She's heading for the basement," said LeWayne.

Mitch saw the end of a single film strip disappear through the doorway leading to the basement. Just ahead of him, LeWayne hit the light switch before heading down. He stopped at the bottom of the steps and Mitch had to maneuver past him to get off the stairs when he caught sight of the mass. It returned to its undulating, shapeless coil of film, a dozen stems extending outward from its core as it hovered in the center of the room above the smeared remnants of Sandy's pentagram. The flapping of plastic tendrils sounded like random whip cracks in the enclosed space.

"Mitch," Kate said. "Look." She gestured to the basement's far wall. "That wasn't there before."

Casting his gaze to where she pointed, Mitch read the single word scrawled on the painted drywall: *HERE*.

He moved to the workbench and retrieved a hammer from the pegboard above the table. The mass shifted as he took a tentative step toward the wall, allowing him to pass.

"Mitch," said Kate. "Be careful."

He gave the wall a few cautious taps, first several feet to the left of the inscription, verifying there was nothing behind it but the building's foundation. Moving to his right, he continued until he heard the unmistakable hollow thump beneath the hammer.

"Bingo."

He swung the hammer with all his strength at the center of the inscription. Its metal claw punched through the drywall and he ripped away a section of the wall, creating an opening over a foot in diameter. Even in the dim light, Mitch could see into the hole, and what was behind it.

"Holy shit."

Wrapped in black plastic and shoved into a space between two wooden slats behind the drywall was what could only be a body. It was covered in dust and appeared to have collapsed in on itself but the shape was unmistakable. Mitch felt his knees weaken

and he braced himself against the wall as LeWayne moved to look.

"It's her, isn't it?" asked Trey.

Mitch nodded. "I think so."

"It has to be," said LeWayne. "All this time, she was right here. She tried to tell me, but I didn't understand." He placed his hand on the wall. "I'm sorry."

Kate put her hand on Sandy's shoulder. "You did it, Sandy. Without you, she might never have been found. Not bad for a witch." Reaching up to wipe tears from her eyes, Sandy sniffled. "Necromancer."

Mitch turned around at the sudden rustling of plastic and saw the mass coming apart. There was no final demonstration, no last messages or other indications of understanding. The coils of film simply went limp, falling lifeless to the basement floor.

"Goodbye, Bettina," LeWayne said. "I hope this means she can finally rest in peace. After all these years, she sure as hell deserves it."

Mitch sighed. "Amen to that."

The projector was the only source of light in the otherwise dark room, but it was enough to illuminate the blood streaking the floor and spattering the walls.

Several of the specks and blotches shivered. They flattened and distended, coming together to form individual shapes which twisted themselves into a set of letters.

WHAT ABOUT ME?

RISE, YE VERMIN!

BETTY ROCKSTEADY

RISE, YE VERMIN!

BETTY ROCKSTEADY

Jenn ignored the cockroach scuttling behind the toilet. The stall door clicked shut and she hopped up, propped Doc Martens on either side of the seat, away from prying eyes. The last showing of *Nightmare on Elm Street 2* trickled out fifteen minutes ago, and Rick would be closing out the register for another twenty at least. Plenty of time for a quick smoke before she started clean-up.

Flame sparked, she exhaled, dared the smoke alarm to go off. She slipped her headphones over her ears and pressed play on the Walkman tucked beneath her uniform. The next song on Christi's mix-tape blared in her ears, *She-Bop*, and Cyndi Lauper's voice drowned out the sound of the door swinging open.

The cockroach shuffled stupidly across the floor and she exhaled smoke at it, frowned. The wings looked... different.

The door *shook,* hard enough to blow a screw from one of the hinges. Jenn screamed and tumbled off the toilet. Her knee hit first, smearing the insect across the filthy floor. Her headphones jolted askew and she heard giggling.

Jenn fumbled the lock, her cheeks blaring nearly as red as her hair. "You scared the shit out of me!"

Christi grinned. "I couldn't find my lighter. I was coming to see if you wanted to run out for a smoke. But here you are, smoking in the bathroom!" She looked Jenn over with flat gray eyes, bit her lip. "And somehow *I'm* the one with the bad reputation."

"Not like Rick would come in here and check on us."

"You never know with that asshole." Christi turned to the wall of mirrors and sinks. She scrunched the ends of her hair and thumbed a cigarette from behind her ear, looked over her shoulder at Jenn. "You're the light of my life."

Jenn tossed her lighter and Christi caught it, lit her smoke and tossed it back in one fluid motion. "He's really been driving me nuts lately." She reached into her purse, pulled out a can of hairspray.

"Watch out there, fire hazard."

Christi rolled her eyes as she fluffed her hair and sprayed.

"When did you grab your purse? Did you clock out already?" Jenn leaned against the sink.

Christi turned to her, pressed her lips together and said, "I'm getting *really* sick of him."

"Yeah, me too." Jenn said. Their shoulders brushed. Christi's teased neon cloud of hair tickled Jenn's cheek. "You'll remember that you dating him was *not* my idea."

"Oh, shut up." Christi stiffened. "He's only here a couple weeks a month with all the cinemas he runs. It

got Mom off my back. I didn't think he'd start getting all hot and heavy with me. I thought he was supposed to be religious or something."

"Wait, hot and heavy?"

"Don't freak out. Nothing happened. He's just giving me those vibes, you know? A man's gotta eat." She tilted her chin and looked up at Jenn, displaying the full effect of her rainy-day eyes. "You're gonna love this. I have a great idea."

"Uh-huh?" Behind Christi, movement caught Jenn's eye as something circled the drain.

Christi said, "I think we should leave tonight." Her face was pale and soft and hopeful, and Jenn reached up to stroke her cheek, ignored the sticky feeling of hairspray.

"I get it. I know how you feel. I know it sucks, but we're so close! Another two paychecks each and we'll really have enough to make it work." She smiled, but Christi didn't smile back. "Come on, I have it all planned out."

"Okay, you know I love your practical nature. And I know you've got it all worked out in your little notebook and that's cool, but... what if we were just ready a little sooner?" Christi's mischievous smile crept across her face, the one that was a little crooked, the one that Jenn loved even though she knew it always meant trouble. "I stole his wallet."

"Christi! You're a common criminal!" She laughed, but it didn't feel right. "You're kidding? We can't do that!"

"Why can't we? I can't *wait* any longer! I really can't! I can't stand the way Mom looks at me every time you call, I can't deal with the rumors and the dirty looks everywhere we go, and I just can't fucking deal with Rick the Prick pawing at me every chance he gets." Tears smudged blue eyeshadow down her cheeks. "I know it was my stupid idea but I thought it would help. Trust me... I feel plenty dumb about it now."

Jenn's flare of anger turned to a searing white light in the shape of Rick's washed-up thirty-something silhouette. "I'm so sorry. I didn't know how bad it was. My parents aren't ever at home, so at least I have somewhere to get away from it." Her hand crept from her lap, towards Christi's knee. "So... we'll just take the cash and leave his ID and family photos and whatever, right?"

The smile that broke through Christi's tears was the glowing orb of the sun evaporating the rain. "The city is gonna change *everything* for us. I'll get a job at a cool arcade and you can do your art and we can go dancing at night and actually *live* our lives instead of hiding in the shadows." The look on Christi's face made her feel like laughing. Nothing was funny, she just wanted to laugh because something amazing was bubbling up.

"I just have to stop home and pack a bag."

"It's in the car. I already packed it for you."

And then that did make Jenn laugh, she couldn't help it, and they were laughing and kissing and their

hands were all over each other when the door swung open again. Christi's face went pale beneath her expertly applied makeup. Jenn turned, surprise quickly replaced by anger.

"I *thought* you girls were taking awhile in here." Rick looked like shit. His skin was sallow and his lips were chapped. The thought of his graceless hands on Christi burned hot rage inside Jenn. His cheek twitched, and behind him, more cockroaches scuttled beneath the door. "You lied right to my face, you fucking bitch."

"Don't you dare call her that." Jenn stood up.

"What, you want to report me to management?" He flicked lanky hair away from his face and nodded to Christi. "Let's go, we've got a conversation to have. I've been working on this for a long time, and I'm not letting you dykes ruin my plans."

"What plans?" Christi's voice sounded raspy. Jenn wanted to turn to her but she didn't want to break eye contact with Rick because he was inching closer somehow, even if she couldn't catch him moving. She put her shoulders back, kept her body between Christi and Rick.

"I said *come on,* Christi."

"She's not going anywhere with you." Behind her, Christi screamed and there was a flutter of something like wings but sharper, an acidic odor, and in the split-second Jenn was distracted, the second her eyes left his face, Rick leapt, and he cupped the back of her skull with his hand and slammed her face into the sink, and everything spun and went black.

A blur of motion. The smell of hairspray. A fading scream.

An impossible amount of pain.

Seconds passed in a dark, thudding heartbeat and Jenn thought *Christi Christi Christi* and she was reaching for her even as she was trying to hold her face together. She needed to find her girlfriend. She needed to fucking kill Rick the Prick, the fucking face-shitting asshole.

Against her better judgment, when she stood, her eyes flickered to her ruined face in the mirror. Even that quick flash of bulging bone and torn flesh made her sick. The vomit tasted like popcorn, and tears and blood and something worse soaked the floor, writhing with *something*. She wavered but instead of falling, she thought *Christi* again and she kept her feet beneath her and looked herself in the eyes when she shoved her jaw back in place.

Jenn spat two teeth into the sink and didn't see the insects crawl from the drain to retrieve them because she was already out the door.

The glare of lights made her wince. The theater foyer smelled of stale popcorn and something else. Something dry, earthy. Lighted frames around movie posters still blinked flashing incantations to the silence. The main theater yawned open to her left, and to her right the concession stand lay abandoned.

There were payphones out front but she only considered them for a second. His office was right *there* and what if he locked the door behind her? Then he'd be in here with Christi and she would be useless, trapped outside until the cops got here and bumbled their way in.

A red handprint smeared black goop across his office door and there was something else, little broken pieces of wings and plastic.

The door handle was still warm, left her hand sticky. She opened the door and dozens of faces leered at her. She jolted back, making her jaw screech with pain.

No. The office was empty but dozens of horror movie posters lined the walls, Freddy Krueger and Michael Myers and aliens with empty eyes. A window that looked out onto a deceptively normal-looking evening was the only break in the macabre faces.

Other than that and a basic desk, chair and filing cabinet, the office was empty.

She felt like she was going to be sick again.

He's got her.

At least the phone was here. Every movement of her head crackled tiny bones in her jaw, ragged shards of glass that threatened to poke through her cheek.

Crawling things scattered when she grabbed the receiver. Filthy fucking place. The phone buzzed a busy signal, again and again, and she jabbed her finger at the button, redialed, dialed home, dialed the pizza place, and busy, and busy, and no help, nowhere, and didn't that buzzing sound like more than a busy signal, didn't it sound like something moving inside the lines?

The useless phone fell to the floor, blared an indignant symphony.

Zombies and maniac killers stared at her across the empty room.

"Where the fuck are you?" The scream ripped a new tear in her cheek, sent a cascade of gore down her uniform.

They must be out in concessions, or in the theater, or *somewhere*, but she felt Christi, she felt like she was close, she *knew* this was where he had taken her and if she didn't find her right fucking *now* something dark in her whispered that she never would.

Still…

Jenn's hand hesitated on the doorknob. She cast one last hopeless glance around the room and the poster for *The Omen* flickered.

More fucking cockroaches were crawling beneath the poster, and yeah, this place was disgusting but that was a *lot* of bugs. Jenn ripped the poster from the wall and beneath it was a smear of something incomprehensible.

Drawn in... blood? No, more textured than blood, somehow worse. Sickening stains of brown and red and black with bits of legs and shells and glittering, torn strips of film roughed out a vertical rectangle, taller than her shadow. Another glob of the disgusting substance smeared an irregular circle midway down the right side, fat and plump like a fist. Like a doorknob.

Jenn's head spun.

Even if this was a door, it would lead to the parking lot out back, it would *have* to.

She swallowed, and her jaw pulsed with pain.

She grabbed the hunk of gore and it moved beneath her hand, twitching insect legs, warm and *soft* and scratching and she turned the knob and something inside her broke when it opened.

The reek of butter and rot. The sound of something shuddering in the darkness. A corridor buzzing with insects, walls winding and twisting towards a distant, sickly light.

One of the bugs spun a lazy circle through the air, landed on her hand. Not a cockroach, but the size of one. Its exoskeleton looked... strange. Plastic. Shiny. Like a crumpled strip of film. And as it moved, she caught a glimpse of a woman's face, her eyes dark with shadow. The insect buzzed back into the air and in the beating of its wings the woman's lips parted and her mouth gaped open.

In the distance, she heard a scream.

Christi.

Jenn's hands sank into the strange flesh of the tunnel. Ahead, glowing lights and posters for movies that could never have existed, strange beating hearts and eyes that looked too familiar.

Bugs swarmed her, their pulsing wings dizzying, their wings whispering to her to shut up and sit down and let this all just be over. She swatted at them uselessly. She ran, kept running, and finally the corridor stopped.

A beautiful, old-fashioned double theater door, much nicer than the ones in Rick's run-down cinema. Next to it, where the movie's poster would normally be, a stained cloth was nailed to the wall. Jenn shook her arm at the insects that covered it until she could read the smears of red and black that screamed the title, *Rise, Ye Vermin!*

The roaches chittered excitedly as Jenn entered the theater. Massive dark curtains covered the most enormous screen she had ever seen. To her left, there were hundreds of seats, and it looked like the theater was almost full, the audience lightly murmuring in a language she didn't understand. An eerie glow leaked from behind the curtains and danced across white faces so quickly she couldn't make out any features.

"You found us! Well, you may as well stay. I don't know what I was thinking. Two virgins are better than one, right?"

Jenn jerked toward his voice. She saw them almost at once, up in the back row, and her stomach sank as her eyes adjusted to the dim light. Rick looked insane in the seeping light that splattered across his face. He had Christi pinned against him in the seat, one of her perfect tits yanked rudely out of her shirt. Jenn couldn't see the look on her face.

"Get the fuck off her!" The words were mangled, her jaw ached with the effort.

"I don't think so. I've put a lot of effort into my virgin-hunting. The horror flicks bring in the teens but how many of them are virgins nowadays? A lot of you chicks just waste my time. I'm sick of you two sneaking around. That means previews are almost over. It's time for the main show."

She finally looked at them. The audience. She was so focused on Christi and Rick but finally she really looked at them and saw why they didn't care what was going on.

They were dead.

Dozens of women in various states of decay twitched and jittered. Jenn stumbled, jolting a fresh new pain through her broken jaw. She tripped into one of the aisle seats and fell into a woman with long, dark hair and a hat. The hat jostled and roaches poured out of her empty eye socket. Jenn barely avoided falling into the corpse's lap as the swarm blasted past her face. She tried to close her eyes but she couldn't look away. In the broken film fluttering of their wings, women ripped hearts from each other's chests and fed them to an inky black *buzzing*.

A guttural scream ripped through her throat. The anger blacked everything else out until she was just rage and pulsing red *pain* and she couldn't handle all this fucking insanity. She could not fucking do this anymore. She screamed again and the pulsing faded, and the chittering of the bugs was replaced by the sound of Christi crying.

Jenn stood up. She pushed her hair out of her face and said, "We're not exactly virgins, you asshole." Ignoring the pain, she poked her tongue between the V of her fingers and Rick cackled with laughter.

She took another step and could see Christi's face clearly now, bruises forming beneath the crimped curtain of her hair, and Rick stood up, pinning her in her seat. He was still laughing. In the darkness of the theater, something quivered behind him.

Jenn vaulted up the last few steps and made it to the back row. Three fresh dead bodies lay between her and her girlfriend. Behind Christi, an empty seat and a clear line to the exit, blocked only by Rick's quivering bulk.

"That doesn't fucking count." Rick's voice was the beating of thousands of wings.

"Oh, it counts." She had to get closer to Christi and that was enough to pull her past the first body, but the corpse *sloshed* when she touched it, and something small flew past her, sharp enough to dribble blood

down her good cheek, enough to make her stumble, to look at the row of moving bodies between her and Rick and hesitate.

He had a knife.

She should have used the payphone outside. What the fuck did she think she was going to do against him? He was bigger and taller and he had Christi and he killed all these girls and now they were going to fucking die in this shitty town and it was all her fault.

Blinking back tears, she met Christi's crazy gray eyes and Christi said "You're the light of my life."

Jenn's hand moved with the practice of reflex. The lighter made a beautiful arc in the flickering light of the theater and landed in Christi's waiting hand.

There was a click as she turned the flame up. "Fuck you!" She sprayed a chemical cloud of hairspray at Rick and sparked the flame.

For a terrible beat, nothing happened.

Then it exploded with a shocking brightness and Rick's cheap uniform burst into flame. His eyes widened in shock and his mouth opened to spurt out a tsunami of insects. A tongue of film escaped his lips, crackling, whispering strange incantations as it bubbled in the heat.

Christi screamed, "This way," and her skinny legs pushed off the seat, spilling her into the spoiled meat of the dead woman next to her. She vaulted over the seats. Jenn followed, tried not to watch as Rick's skin blistered. He grabbed her arm as she passed, and she felt the heat of the flame. Jenn ripped herself away from him and his skin spilled open, the scent of rot and vinegar and burning as he was torn apart.

A massive spool of film spat from his body, snapped tight around Jenn's wrist, tried to yank her into Christi's recently vacated seat. It burned her skin where it touched. Roaches clustered over her face and tickled at her mouth. A gust of foul air billowed through the theater and an unholy light spilled inside as the curtains slowly inched apart.

Christi screamed. Jenn turned to see her by the exit sign. She ripped the film from her wrist and kept her eyes on Christi's face. She ran.

The screen whispered her name and the fire licked at her neck and the film twisted around her legs, caressed her like a lover as the bugs beat at her back. She fell into Christi's arms just for a second, just long enough to inhale the singed chemical smell of her hair. Corpses shuddered and tumbled from their seats and the crawling bits of film crumpled and burned.

A sound like a great intake of breath, curtains groaning, a light that sickened the air as the flame spread.

They ran.

A few stray bugs still crawled through the corridor, but they seemed listless. Broken. *The Omen* poster fluttered softly behind them and they fell into uneasy neon silence.

Christi's face crumpled, reached for Jenn's ruined cheek, pale hand trembling inches from the heat of the pain and Jenn grabbed her hand and kissed it and then they didn't stop running until they were outside.

Rain pounded from the sky and washed blood onto the pavement. Christi slipped under Jenn's arm and guided her towards the employee parking lot out back.

"You okay?" Jenn rasped. Christie looked up at her, bangs pasted to her forehead, bruises along the curves of her face, a smile erupting slowly into laughter.

So fucking beautiful.

"*What*?" Jenn was already laughing too.

"I just..." Christie giggled as she pulled out the car keys for her AMC Eagle. "I don't feel so bad about stealing his wallet now, ya know?" She unlocked Jenn's door first. They were both still giggling a little when the flaming theater disappeared into the horizon behind them.

THE
CRONENBERG
CONCERTO

KEITH FERRELL

THE CRONENBERG CONCERTO

KEITH FERRELL

I t should have been a golden age.

The 80s should have been the most blood-red golden age ever for the movies Lee loved and lived for.

But it wasn't.

Even after a midnight movie, the theaters today were too clean for him.

The seats were too comfortable, the popcorn (not that he ever ordered popcorn anymore) too fresh.

The floors weren't sticky; the bathrooms weren't stained; the screens weren't torn and spotted.

The projectors were too reliable, not to mention the projectionists. Lee couldn't remember the last time a film had broken or a projector bulb burned out.

The audiences were not the audiences Lee wished to sit with. They offered no companionship, no shared experience; their attendance brought neither prospect nor potential. Like the theaters they filled, the audiences were too clean.

The movies themselves were too clean. Not that he wanted filth. Not sex-filth, anyway. There was nothing prurient about either his interest or his attendance. Lee disliked the nudity and increasingly explicit sexuality that began creeping onto the screen during the 70s and became a torrent by the turn of the new decade. He came to see skin flayed not bared, yet most of the movies now were more bare than bloody.

That wasn't what he had come to see since he was a kid in the 60s, when the movies he loved were born. He'd been present at their birth, and he'd watched them grow over the twenty years since. He'd seen them all, though only a very few achieved the greatness that earned his highest tribute and homage.

There was nothing in the theaters for Lee anymore, and yet he still came. He could not stop or would not. He stood in line—sometimes they were long, sometimes the theaters sold out their midnight shows, and not just for *Rocky Horror*, that abomination, that musical mockery of all that drew him, all that he came for, all that had drawn him for decades.

He knew what he came to find, and not just on the screen. What he came for was what he had been coming for since he was ten, yet found so rarely on the screens anymore. Nor was there much of what he wanted in the seats around him, even when a theater was full.

Some of the other patrons noticed Lee, though not many. Lost in their own heads, most of those heads addled by pot or worse, another gift of the 60s that persisted and proliferated into the 80s. Sometimes they even burned a joint in the theater. The odor made Lee want to throw up and sometimes he did.

Some who noticed him looked away. One or two would stare. Occasionally he would overhear a couple, out for a Friday or Saturday night date, whisper to each other about *that poor man.*

The ticket booth attendants noticed too, and the ticket-takers inside. How could they not when he fumbled with his wallet, or extended his ticket between the two fingers that were all that remained on his right hand?

He ignored their whispers and paid no attention to their averted gazes. Let them whisper and look away. They weren't what he came to see.

But less and less did the screens offer what he came to see either.

Some golden age.

Had he given twenty years of himself for *this*—standing in line at a nice theater with a nice, if stoned, audience, to see a movie that whatever its title and advertising promised would be nice in its own way, filled with special effects that everyone in the theater knew weren't real?

It was the way of the world now, and Lee hated it. This was not what he'd lived for since the summer of '63.

That summer was the best of his life. He'd always heard you never forget your first time, and that summer proved it.

There were two theaters in the small town where his family lived when he was ten. The Movietime was the respectable theater, spotless and inviting on the main street of the town's business district. Sometimes Lee's mom or dad would drop him and his brother off there for a Saturday matinee, a Disney flick, cowboy movie or a kiddie comedy. Nothing was at risk in any of those movies. Nothing in any of them spoke to Lee.

The other theater, the Superb, was in a bad neighborhood fourteen blocks from Lee's house. Lee's mother never dropped her children off there and avoided even driving through that part of town.

The Superb was a little grindhouse fallen on hard times even for a grindhouse. Lee was ten when he snuck out of the house on a Sunday afternoon, his parents napping after the heavy Sunday dinner that followed an equally heavy Sunday at the church his mother insisted they attend.

Lee dozed through the sermon. As usual, he had stayed up late Saturday night to catch the week's *Terror Theater* on channel 8. The channel didn't come in well, and Lee had to watch with the sound turned way down to keep from waking his parents. They wouldn't approve of him being up so late, and they *sure* wouldn't approve of what he was watching. Lee didn't approve of what he was watching either.

In the first place, the show had a host, some local TV weatherman who dressed up on Saturday nights in a top hat and black cape, fake fangs giving him a lisp, fake Bela Lugosi accent giving Lee the willies and not out of fear or anything close to it. For his Saturday

night dress up duties, the weatherman called himself Doctor U. N. Dertaker. His spiel was as corny as his name. Lee hardly listened to the clown's patter of recycled jokes ("Frankenstein, Wolfman and Dracula walk into a bar...") and horrid puns ("The Wolfman's Number One with a Bullet—a *Silver* Bullet!"). He just wanted the guy to get on with the movies. The movies were what Lee stayed up for.

Most of them weren't worth it, not even close. Third-rate B-movies from the 40s (*The Ape, The Mad Monster*), the 50s (*Bride of the Gorilla, The Giant Gila Monster*), and occasionally something from the 60s (*The Brain That Wouldn't Die, The Beast of Yucca Flats*). Bad movies even by the standards of bad movies.

But Lee stayed up, crouching close to the TV, wiggling the rabbit ears for better reception, hoping for some sort of reward for his effort.

Occasionally he found what he wanted, *Terror Theater*'s syndicated package of movies providing a *Freaks* or *Horror of Dracula* for every fifteen or twenty *Attack of the Crab Monsters* or *Creature with the Atom Brain*.

It wasn't enough, and the good movies were censored even before the prints got to the station. One or two of them—notably *Horror of Dracula* and the other Hammer films that somehow found their way into the rotation—raised an outcry from concerned parents groups, resulting in an on-air apology from none other than Doctor U. N. Dertaker, who proved as unconvincing in contrition as comedy.

The *Terror Theater* movie the night before the day Lee's life changed was *The Neanderthal Man*, a 1953 piece of crap, but Lee stayed with it all the way. It was a discipline with him, not yet a ritual. That would come later.

The fact that the movie was made the year he was born played a part, too. He was determined to see every horror movie made in 1953, and he was delighted to be able to check *The Neanderthal Man* off his list.

During the commercials and the weatherman's awful hosting, Lee planned his Sunday escape. He'd seen the Superb's ad in the paper that morning and it was all he thought about. You had to look hard to find the ad, hidden in the sports pages which held little interest for Lee. He had no idea why he was looking in that section that Saturday, but on those rare occasions when he allowed himself to feel that there was some order and purpose to the universe, Lee thought he must have been guided to it.

Mostly he felt it was the luckiest break of his life. The ad's headline grabbed him and had not let him go:

NOTHING SO APPALLING IN THE ANNALS OF HORROR!

He had to stop for a moment to think about what *appalling* might mean. The more he thought the more convinced he was that it meant that the kind of movie he'd looked for all his life had come to town.

He was going to see it.

He was going to see it tomorrow. There was a three o'clock show and if he played things right, he would be there to see for himself just what *appalling* meant.

His parents stretched out for their naps after the big Sunday lunch. Lee waited as long as he could to leave and still make it to the Superb.

He barely got there in time and was still breathing hard after chaining his bike to a lamppost just down the street. His shirt was sticky with sweat and his heart pounded wildly as he stepped up to the ticket booth. The old guy in the booth was chewing on the stub of an unlit cigar. He looked at Lee and yawned. "No kids allowed," he said.

Lee expected that and had a plan. Tickets were fifty cents. He pushed two dollar bills—damp from his sweaty jeans—at the man and said, "No change, please."

That got the guy's attention. He shot a glance up and down the street. There was no one in sight. He took Lee's two bucks and said, "Anybody catches you, you snuck in, got me?"

Lee nodded, took his ticket and entered the theater.

It was dim in the lobby, not like the bright entrance to the Movietime. A bulb flickered over the concession stand whose glass front was smudged. The guy from the ticket booth came in and asked if Lee wanted anything.

Lee shook his head; that two dollars was all he had. The guy sighed and gestured toward the door to the auditorium. "Get in and keep your mouth shut."

Lee walked to the door and pulled it open. The auditorium was dimmer than the lobby and Lee waited a moment for his eyes to adjust. When he could see, he walked slowly down the right side of the theater, the soles of his Keds making a squicky sound with each step.

There were only three other people in the theater, one of them snoring. Lee found a seat far from them and close to the front. He sat down just before the screen came to life.

Within minutes, Lee knew what *appalling* meant.

He'd never seen anything like this, and soon learned that he had never seen anything like it because there had never *been* anything like it before.

This wasn't *Terror Theater* crap.

This wasn't *Frankenstein* or *The Wolfman* or even *Freaks*.

This wasn't Hammer horror with its English accents and clean clothes and civilized acting.

This was the real thing, realer than anything Lee had ever experienced. This was what he wanted all along. He hadn't known he could want anything so much.

By the time the movie ended, Lee was ready to stay through it again, to stay through all the showings. But he knew he couldn't. He had to get home. As the last of the movie faded, he paid his tribute and rushed from the theater, unchained his bike and pedaled furiously home. His parents were upset when he came in, but he

planned for this too, and told them he was late because he had a bike accident. He was able to calm them down without giving any hint of where he was or what he had seen. They wouldn't understand. They would be *appalled*. Lee kept his mouth shut and not just for his parents' sake.

He didn't sleep that night. When he closed his eyes, he was able to relive every minute of *Blood Feast*.

He wanted to see it again, but it left town before his mother would even think about letting him get back on his bike. He didn't argue. He kept his mouth shut and his eyes open, searching for the Superb's ads every Saturday when the new movies came out.

The Superb came through twice more that year, *Dementia 13* and *Paranoiac*, though neither came close to giving Lee what *Blood Feast* provided, neither inspired him to worship. He saw *Paranoiac*, a decent British flick, but not nearly enough blood.

The Superb closed in the summer of '64 but that was okay. His family moved to the city that summer, and the city had more theaters, three of them grinders, one of which he could reach on his bike. The other two required bus rides. Mostly he came home disappointed, his desire for worship undiminished but unconsummated. That was all right—he was learning to live with disappointment. It made the fulfillment all the sweeter when he did receive a gift from the screen. Lee found a few of those gifts over the course of the 60s, including two more from the master, *Two Thousand Maniacs!* and, best of all, *Color Me Blood Red.* He honored them with worship and ritual. Almost as good, even though black-and-white, was *Night of the Living Dead*, although by the time that came out the potheads were coming out too.

The deepening recessive 70s and the collapse of the inner cities that came with them were boom times for Lee. The three downtown theaters that had drawn date night couples to Doris Day and Rock Hudson, and families to *Mary Poppins* and *The Sound of Music*, and everybody to John Wayne or Jerry Lewis or Elvis movies found themselves unable to attract even a fraction of their former audiences. Those audiences moved to the suburbs and took their moviegoing habits with them. A night out at the movies meant a night out at the mall or the multiplex where you could take your choice of four or five or even six movie screens. Doris Day and Rock Hudson gave way to Paul Newman and Robert Redford, Elvis yielded the box office to Burt Reynolds, Jerry Lewis to Steve Martin. John Wayne persisted. None of them showed up on downtown screens anymore.

Lacking a respectable trade, the downtown theater operators turned to less than respectable movies. The Rialto did good business with Blaxploitation flicks, which held little interest for Lee, (although he did catch *Blacula* but its horrors didn't particularly catch him; *Sugar Hill's* zombies had their moments and he caught

it on a double-feature with *Black Godfather*, which wasn't his cup of blood at all).

He had far better luck at the Nevis and the Showplace.

Built in the 50s, the Nevis specialized in kung fu films, but an occasional horror movie crept in. When one did, Lee was there. Most of the horrors that played at the Nevis were crap, and the rituals Lee performed there were minor, though never perfunctory.

The Showplace, though, was a palace from the 20s. For a half century, it was the biggest and fanciest and most elegant theater in town, and boasted the biggest screen in the whole state. It hung on until '69, but when it went, it went fast—its owners dumping the theater for a song to a couple of kids in their twenties who looked the other way when their audiences toked up. Some said you could buy pot at the concession stand along with popcorn and candy. Lee didn't know whether that was true, and he didn't care. The Showplace booked films that drew that sort of audience, and some of those were films whose gifts drew Lee.

It was at the Showplace where the 70s started for Lee with one of the greatest of those gifts, *Bloodthirsty Butchers*, a work of genius in Lee's eyes, almost beyond belief in the purity of what it brought to the enormous Showplace screen. He felt the way he had when he saw *Blood Feast*. This was what he was looking for. This was what he worshipped. A teenager now, driving and better able to get out and around and see movies more than once, Lee saved his ritual for his third viewing of *Butchers* and timed it to match the scene that most inspired him.

Once he was able to drive, he had a long, fitful relationship with drive-ins. There were five in the city when his family moved there, but only three were still in operation when he turned sixteen and got his driver's license. He went to each of them when a title promised the possibility of worship. He found what he was looking for only a couple of times at drive-ins, most notably a showing of *I Spit on Your Grave* in '79. He was in his mid-twenties by then, living on his own, able to see whatever he wanted whenever he wanted. The movie had too much sex for Lee's taste, but it had blood too, and he judged it worthy of ritual. But there was an emptiness to ritual performed alone in a car, with other audience members sealed in their own cars, insulated. The drive-in closed later that year, and Lee never went to an outdoor movie again.

And now it was the 80s, the golden age that wasn't.

The drive-ins were gone. The Nevis and the Rialto and even the Showplace were all gone too, the Rialto razed, the Showplace shuttered, the Nevis converted into a video store of all things.

The 'plexes were all that remained. And while they showed more horror movies than ever, fewer and fewer of them offered anything for Lee to worship.

The movies were in many ways bloodier than ever, but it was Hollywood blood.

The acting was far better than ever, but that was because the movies starred actors, people you could see in other movies that weren't horror.

The directors were better than ever because they were film school graduates, professionals.

It was the professionalism that bothered Lee the most. There was nothing authentic about most of the movies that promised horror and blood and gore. There was nothing for Lee in the *Halloweens* or the *Friday the 13ths* or any of the rest of the stupid teen massacre movies with their programmed hackings and slashings. There was even less in the *Exorcists* and *Poltergeists* and *Shinings* with their huge budgets and big-name actors. It was all product, manufactured on assembly lines to fill screens in clean well-lit theaters, no different, really, from Elvis or Burt Reynolds or John Wayne movies.

There was nothing to inspire Lee.

There was nothing that spoke to him.

There was nothing *appalling* in the way that the real things appalled and lifted him out of himself.

Real things were still being made, but the realest of them never made it to the theaters. They went straight to tape. Tape was how he saw *Cannibal Holocaust* a couple of years ago, and that was real. But while video could provide what he looked for, watching it on television couldn't. He never performed his rituals at home. The ritual was meant for theaters, and not the sorts of theaters that played movies these days.

Nevertheless, he took his place in line at the movie-plex. He had some hope as he waited to buy his ticket. The guy who made the movie had been real once and one of his movies, *Rabid*, inspired a ritual. But that was in '77, six years ago, and Lee caught it at nearly the last gasp of the *Nevis*. Since then the director had gotten more respectable and less real. Lee had seen it happen before. Just last year the guy who made *Texas Chainsaw*—one of the all-time greats and one of the greatest ritual experiences of Lee's life, even though the movie had less blood than you'd think—made *Poltergeist*, Hollywood crap all the way through and not a scare in it.

Lee worried that the guy who made *Rabid* would go the same way. Two years ago, he'd turned out for *Scanners,* and while it had its moments—Lee thought it would be a ritual for the ages if he could make his head explode—it wasn't worthy of even a small ritual. Maybe tonight would be different, he thought as he moved to the ticket booth.

"One for *Videodrome*," he said, extending a ten between his two fingers. As always when he spoke there was a reaction. He caught a flash of concern or revulsion from the girl selling tickets. He paid her no more mind than he did the kid behind him who looked at the left side of Lee's face and whispered, "*van Gogh,*" to his date who shushed him even as she laughed.

Lee went into the theater and found his seat.

The movie was better than *Scanners,* though not nearly real enough for a ritual. But it gave Lee something to think about. With its vision of video consuming the world, how could it not? Video was too easy, too convenient. You didn't have to work to see a video, you didn't have to make an effort to seek out what you wanted. You didn't have to go into a dark place to see it. There was no ritual to watching a video. It wasn't real.

Without irony he drove downtown and stopped at what the marquee now proclaimed was Nevis Video. Whoever owned it put in some money and effort to make the place appealing. The store was nearly as clean and well-lit as the multiplex at the mall, and even had a concession counter, its glass front polished and free of smudges. The popcorn smelled fresh. The video selection was broad and eclectic.

Lee walked to the horror section and drew a breath as he scanned the titles. There among the phony stuff stood video cassette cases holding the films he'd worshipped for twenty years. Even encased in plastic they spoke to him, giving their own thanks for the gifts he gave them.

He'd bitten off the tip of his tongue as he watched *Blood Feast* and left it on the floor of the Superb.

He'd smuggled a razor-sharp knife into his second viewing of *Bloodthirsty Butchers* and used it to remove his left nipple at precisely the moment when a breast was revealed beneath the crust of a meat pie.

He'd cut off the first of his fingers at *Living Dead* with pruning shears, and to add flavor to the homage, he'd chewed on the finger a bit before depositing it on the floor of the Nevis.

He hacked off his ear at *Texas Chainsaw* and dropped it to the Showtime's sticky carpet where, he was almost positive, a rat carried it off.

He'd sliced open his armpit at *Rabid* and let the blood soak into the seat next to him.

He looked at the other titles and thought of what they'd given him and all the parts of himself he'd given them in return.

All the movies that spoke were here, their voices imprisoned on videotape now, no more real than anything else in the store.

People would rent them and take them home, and play them, perhaps rewinding the most appalling parts—but laughing as they did so. Because it wouldn't be real to them. They wouldn't be appalled. They would be amused.

It was too easy.

He thought of the movie he just saw and realized it was only going to get easier.

There would come a time, Lee thought with a clarity so sudden and complete that he took it for a revelation.

There would come a time when you wouldn't have to go to a store, much less a theater, to see these movies.

They would come straight to you at home somehow, beamed right at you like something on *Star Trek*.

They would be even less real than they were on tape.

There was nothing he could do to stop it. He knew that much.

The world he belonged to was no longer real, and never would be again.

He felt a sense of loss almost as profound in its devastating way as the sense of exaltation he'd felt seeing the movies in dark, sticky, malodorous theaters.

Where they were *real.*

Where they belonged.

Where *he* belonged.

After a moment, Lee stepped into the restroom where he tore the nail from one of his fingers.

He dropped it on the floor in front of the horror section.

It was not an act of worship.

Lee left the store without renting anything.

CREATURE
FEATURE

GARY JONAS

CREATURE FEATURE

GARY JONAS

F ade in on the Scheherazade Palace in Los Viejos, Colorado, an old movie theater that closed its doors to the public in the summer of 1956. The marquee displayed *Earth vs. the Flying Saucers,* though a few of the letters went missing over the years. Posters from the last time the theater was open still adorned the walls letting people know *War and Peace* and *Bus Stop* were "coming soon."

The box office window had an old, faded sign that read, *Permanently Closed for Business.*

Word on the street was they held private screenings twenty-four hours a day that played to an empty house, or the Illuminati with devil worshippers sacrificed virgins at every showing. Most folks just figured Old Man Jenkins had finally gone off his rocker, but he could afford to do whatever he wanted.

On Monday, July 1, 1985, the Palace was added to Mark Lassiter's delivery route. The dock foreman refused to tell Mark why he was assigned a sixteen-foot refrigerated truck to deliver to an abandoned movie theater. Instead, the foreman just ran through the special protocols Mark had to follow, and said Old Man Jenkins was the most important client they had, and to not screw it up the way Tom had.

Mark climbed into the truck. A square box, eighteen inches on each side, sat on the passenger seat with a packing slip listing the titles of the movie canisters within. Some of them were opening in the next week, but some weren't supposed to hit theaters until later that month: *Back to the Future, Red Sonja, The Emerald Forest, Mad Max Beyond Thunderdome, Silverado, Dr. Otto and the Riddle of the Gloom Beam.* The other titles were in foreign languages.

He rolled down his window and waved to the foreman. "Shouldn't this box be in the back?"

The foreman shook his head. "Jenkins likes to get the movies first, so they ride up front. Now go make that delivery and get your ass back here. Your regular truck will be waiting for you. This truck is exclusively used for Mr. Jenkins."

"Why?"

"Because he pays a lot of money. Now get going. You can't be late."

Mark patted the box, and turned the key in the ignition. The engine purred, and the big truck handled like a dream, unlike every other vehicle he'd driven for Davis Deliveries.

Mark drove straight to the Palace.

He wheeled around to the back alley entrance as instructed. A massive electric fence stood guard with warnings to any who approached that touching the

gate could lead to permanent injury or death. He got the remote from the glovebox, pressed the button, and waited as the gate swung inward.

He pulled through, and parked at the delivery door as the gate closed.

Mark climbed out of the truck as the delivery door creaked open, and a woman in her late twenties stepped outside. She wore tight blue jeans and a white button up shirt. Her brown hair tumbled over her shoulders, and her blue eyes locked onto Mark's in a way he mistook for attraction.

"You're Tom's replacement?" she asked.

"Mark," he said, nodding. "What's your name?"

"Tanya. Did they give you the rundown?"

"Be on time, don't knock."

"No," she said, leaning in the doorway. "The rules for the deliveries."

He gave her a confused look. "Better tell me yourself."

"Do you have your NDA?"

"No."

She sighed. "Wait right here. I'll go get one. You'll need to sign it before we go any further."

She closed the door.

A few minutes later, she returned with several sheets of paper and a pen.

"It's standard," she said. "You can't tell anyone what you see or hear inside. If you reveal anything at all, you'll answer to Sheriff Jones."

Mark skimmed the NDA, and it seemed pretty standard, until under Obligations of Receiving Party, he read: *Penalties for disclosure include prison with a minimum sentence of ten years for minor infractions, up to permanent termination of all life functions and forfeiture of soul until the end of time.*

He pointed to the clause. "Is this some kind of joke?"

She gazed at him, bored. "What part?"

"This says I can be killed if I talk."

She nodded. "That's correct."

"Tom signed this?"

"He did," she said.

Mark frowned. "Tom died in a car wreck on Saturday. There wasn't enough of him left to bury."

She shrugged. "Clearly unrelated, so you won't have any hesitation signing it."

"This won't hold up in court."

She handed him the pen, expressionless.

"Do you always take the deliveries?" he asked.

"Monday through Friday."

He signed the form and handed it back. She held out her hand for the pen, and he returned that, too.

He winked. "Then I guess we'll be seeing a lot of each other."

She didn't react. Instead, she said, "When you arrive, you are not to enter the theater. Do not look behind the curtains. Wheel the dolly to the concession stand, load the crates into the freezer, and place the box of movie

canisters on the counter. Then take the old crates back to your truck."

"And the old movie canisters?"

"Leave those. We keep stock of every film we've shown here since 1956."

"That seems excessive."

"Our clients sometimes request repeat screenings of their favorite films."

"Interesting."

"No matter what you hear behind the curtains, do not enter the theater. Got it?"

He leaned closer. "If I slip you ten bucks, can I sneak in to see *Back to the Future* early? We could watch it together. Maybe share some popcorn?"

"You can watch it when it opens at the Starlight like everyone else."

"You get to see it today, though, right?"

"I have to change the reels."

She propped the door open and he carried the box of movies inside.

The walls, floors, and ceilings were covered with black carpet. At the end of the hall, a red curtain separated the theater from the lobby. He heard gunshots, and figured they were screening an action movie or a western. An odd aroma drifted through the curtains.

"What is that smell?"

"Keep moving," Tanya said.

There was nothing in the lobby except the concession stand and three stacks of large silver crates that Mark thought would make great footlockers.

The popcorn machine was empty. There wasn't a soda machine, or any candy, or hot dogs. Just a counter with large, black trays.

Behind the counter, a massive steel door led to a freezer.

Tanya followed and when Mark set the box of movies on the counter, she opened it.

"Popcorn machine busted or something?" he asked.

"Our clients have other appetites. Go get the crates."

Mark went out to the truck and opened the back. Two rows of silver crates like those in the lobby stood waiting to be unloaded. A dolly lay on the floor.

He brought in the new crates, and loaded up the empties, but they rattled when he tipped them onto the dolly.

"What's in these?" he asked.

"Trays," Tanya said, pointing at the black plates on the counter. "And some trash. You signed the NDA, so feel free to take a look."

Mark opened the crate and saw T-bones, remains of chicken breasts, drumsticks, and pork ribs with dirty trays. He wrinkled his nose at the smell and closed the lid. The meat looked uncooked.

"Your clientele likes raw meat?"

"It's a delicacy to some."

He unloaded the rest of the new crates and loaded the returns.

"Thanks for your help," Tanya said at the delivery door.

"It's been weird," he said.

She finally gave him a genuine smile. "Weird is normal here."

He handed her the clipboard to sign for the delivery. "Just sign here," he said, pointing. "Any chance you're free for dinner sometime this week?"

She signed the board, and handed it back, still grinning. "Let me think about it."

Dinner on Saturday was delicious, and Tanya was more open and friendly, but she mostly talked movies. She mentioned so many science fiction films that Mark took her for a drive down Highway 17, locally known as the Cosmic Highway due to so many UFO sightings. They parked in the middle of nowhere. It was a little chilly, but not to the point where he needed to turn on the heater. They reclined the car seats, sat close, and shared some body heat.

"I have to warn you," she said, gazing at the sky, "my life revolves around movies."

"I like movies," Mark said. "I thought you might want to talk about something that wasn't work-related, though."

"Work is my life. We perform an important service to the world."

Mark laughed.

"You don't think entertainment is important?"

"Oh, it is," he said. He pointed to the sky. "Look, a shooting star."

Tanya leaned her head against Mark's shoulder. He put an arm around her, and she didn't pull away. Maybe there was such a thing as Hollywood love. He just needed a good soundtrack, so he reached over, and clicked on the radio. "You Spin Me Round (Like a Record)" by Dead or Alive blasted from the speakers. Mark turned the volume down, and punched a button to scan to the next station. "Don't You (Forget About Me)" by Simple Minds came on. Tanya cuddled closer. The right music made a difference.

"I loved *The Breakfast Club,*" she said, "but I don't want to go back to high school. I'd rather we drove around like Holly and Kit in *Badlands*. Or maybe *Bonnie and Clyde*."

"Or maybe we could pick a movie where we both get to live," Mark said.

"Were you friends with Tom?" she asked.

"Nah. He was a dick," he said.

"Good. Don't do like he did," she said.

"What did he do?"

"He was late for a delivery. I like you, Mark. So please, don't ever be late."

"I like seeing you. I'll never be late for that."

"Even if you're sick. Please don't be late. We can't accept any excuses."

"Yeah, I got it the first time."

"If the clients don't like something, we have to change the movie quickly or they get upset. And believe me, you don't want to see them upset."

"Bad for business?" Mark asked.

"Bad for everyone."

"All right," he said, stroking her hair. "I won't be late. So, what are your favorite movies?"

"My favorites are the ones our patrons can watch over and over again. *Star Wars, Invasion of the Body Snatchers, Laserblast, Raiders of the Lost Ark, Phantasm,* and *Jaws,* though they tend to root for the shark."

"I totally get *Star Wars* and *Raiders*, but *Laserblast?*"

"When humans are ruled by aliens, they appreciate that."

"Odd clients," Mark said.

"They aren't from around here," she said, taking a deep breath. "Never mind. You'd think I'm crazy."

"No, not at all. I think you're great."

Tanya blushed.

"Have you ever read anything by H.P. Lovecraft?" she asked.

"Can't say I have."

"He wrote about the Elder Gods. 'The Call of Cthulhu' and such."

"Go on," he said.

"Well, the Elder Gods, or the Old Ones as they're sometimes called, they're...they're real. They devour bodies and souls, but my grandfather learned that they were distracted by movies. We've trapped them in the theater, and keep their attention by giving them a steady diet of stories and flesh. Otherwise... we're all doomed."

Even in the dark, Mark could tell she was serious, but she was also a little bundle of hotness, and while the crazy kept rising on the charts, he was horny, and now that the radio was playing "In the Air Tonight" by Phil Collins, he thought he could be Tom Cruise to her Rebecca De Mornay. Loving her might be worth some *Risky Business*, he thought, and moved to kiss her.

"That's why you can't ever be late," she said, avoiding his lips. "While they sometimes request repeat showings, we need new movies to show them. All the time."

"What if the projector breaks?" he asked, tossing some logic into the conversation.

"We have backups. Projectors, bulbs, two extra generators in case of power outages. We've got it covered," she said, which under other circumstances might sound rational, but she followed it up with another batch of insanity. "The fate of the world depends on us keeping them riveted to the screen. We feed them raw meat, and the occasional human who screws up. Like my mother, who sacrificed herself when the film broke during *Alien*."

"That sounds awful," Mark said, wondering if he should give up and just take her home. The hotness chart didn't have room for this much crazy.

"I know," she said. "The film broke right as the alien burst from John Hurt's chest. Your coworker, Tom, he was an hour late. We were supposed to get an advance copy of *Explorers*, and he gave a sad excuse about his mother being rushed to the hospital. What's one life compared to billions? We managed to get *The Rocky Horror Picture Show* up and running before they escaped the theater. They love that movie, so we keep it accessible, but they prefer it Saturday nights at midnight. When Tom showed up, we fed him to the Old Ones. I don't want to have to do that to you, Mark, but as they say, *the show must go on*."

Her tone was sincere. "Fascinating," Mark said, raising an eyebrow like Mr. Spock.

"That's nothing compared to the busloads of people we bring in once a month. The Old Ones devour souls, you see, and..." She kept talking, but he'd finally heard enough.

Mark sat up, and looked around.

"What are you doing?" she asked.

"Looking for Allen Funt. There has to be a camera crew around here trying to see how much nonsense I'll listen to before they tell me I'm on some *Candid Camera* special."

"You don't believe me?" she asked.

"I'm sorry, but no. Not a word. Anyhow, it's getting late and I've got an early morning."

Mark arrived on time Monday morning, and Tanya glared at him when he brought in the crates.

"Follow me," she said.

"I have other deliveries to make."

"Don't talk," she said. "In fact, don't even whisper."

She grabbed him by the hand, and dragged him through a set of red curtains leading into a short hallway to reveal a gap of about three feet before another curtain separated them from the theater. The odd smell intensified, but he couldn't place it. On the left wall, a door led to the projection room.

Tanya guided him inside, then leaned close and whispered, "Look out the window at the audience."

Mark rolled his eyes, but did as she said. He slipped around the projector, which clicked along throwing a Chinese chop-chop movie on the screen.

He leaned close to the window, and put his hand up to block his reflection for a better view into the theater.

A face with too many eyes stared back at him, and a mouth with far too many sharp teeth opened and smacked against the glass, scratching it.

Mark jumped back, but Tanya put her hands on his shoulders to keep him from falling.

"What the fuck is that?"

"Shh. Go back to the glass," she whispered. "That one is just curious, but it can't break through, and it will settle down now that it knows you're here."

He eased himself back to the glass, and the creature slid into its seat. Row after row of dark and slimy crea-

tures gazed enraptured at the kung fu dancing on the screen. Tentacles waved. Tongues slurped. Some of the Old Ones had scales. Some sported manes of wild hair and antennae. Others had eyestalks growing out of their heads and wings sprouting from their shoulders.

"My grandfather is about to feed them. Most snack breaks are just dead animals, but I had him move up the main course for your edification."

Mark started to speak, but she put a finger to his lips.

"Don't worry," she said, "they're sedated."

A side door opened, spilling yellow light onto the front rows. Old Man Jenkins wheeled in a gurney that held an elderly naked man.

He parked the gurney at one end of the row and motioned for the creatures to remain seated. He rushed out, then returned a moment later with another gurney holding a naked woman.

Eventually four *snacks* took up the gap between the front row and the screen.

Old Man Jenkins let himself out as the credits started to roll.

Tanya grabbed a microphone, and spoke into it. "Snack break for five minutes while we change the film. Our next feature is *Invasion U.S.A.* starring Chuck Norris."

She pointed at the glass, and pushed Mark forward.

When the credits ended, the creatures pounced upon their meals. They bit off heads, ripped bodies apart, and passed arms, legs, and torsos for the others to share.

Mark's stomach flipped and Tanya handed him a bucket.

"They're all terminally ill patients from hospice centers in the region," she said, offering him a rag to wipe the vomit from his lips.

Mark couldn't speak. He focused on keeping the contents of his stomach in the bucket.

She got the Chuck Norris movie prepped and said, "You can go now. And while it should go without saying, don't be late, or they'll be dining on a healthier, younger snack."

The next day, Tanya was waiting outside when Mark pulled up in the delivery truck.

"I thought you might quit," she said.

"Bills to pay," he said.

"You're the only living outsider to ever witness the devouring of souls."

"It was terrible."

"Small price to pay to keep the world safe. You do understand that's what we're doing, right?"

"I considered going to the sheriff," Mark said.

"He knows all about it. When we don't have enough hospice patients, he brings us criminals from the penitentiary. He says they're on death row, but I don't know. There've been a lot of them."

"You're okay with this?" he asked.

"If not for my family, and others like us around the world, the Old Ones would have already feasted on every soul on the planet."

This time, Mark believed her.

A few weeks later, life threw Mark a curveball. He started his route five minutes late, and didn't get across the railroad tracks before the train arrived. It shouldn't have been an issue, but he stopped too close to a station wagon in front, and a Corvette practically drove up his tailpipe. There wasn't room to get turned around without hitting another vehicle. "The Power of Love" by Huey Lewis and the News played on the radio.

Mark kept looking at his watch. If he didn't get moving soon, he might be late for the delivery. He didn't have a time-traveling DeLorean, and Tanya told him they were on a tight schedule because the clients knew *Re-Animator* was going to be delivered. They *really* wanted to see it.

Traffic was backed up and there was nowhere to go. While he didn't believe the fate of the world rested on his delivery because Tanya could start another movie, he knew they wouldn't forgive him for being late. Mark couldn't wait any longer. He wheeled the truck off the road, clipping the station wagon because he didn't want to crunch the Corvette.

The driver of the station wagon got out of his vehicle and gave him the finger, but Mark just waved, and gunned the engine. There wasn't any traffic going back the way he came.

If he took Turner Avenue to Ward Street, he might be able to go around the train. It was his only hope.

Turner Avenue was clear, and he made good time, but the route took him a mile out of the way. Finally, he found a street that went through, and he swung onto Main Street. He checked his watch. It all depended on the lights.

Mark ran three red lights, and pulled up to the theater two minutes late. Tanya leaned against the door, checking her watch as he hopped out of the truck.

"That was a close one," Mark said.

"You're late," she said.

"Traffic," Mark said, shrugging.

"Give me the movies," she said.

He got the box out of the truck and handed it to her.

She ripped the flaps open, dug through the canisters to find *Re-Animator* and let out a sigh of relief.

"Get unloaded," she said. "I'm going to get this spooled up."

Once Mark was done, he went back inside with his clipboard for her signature, but she wasn't in the lobby.

There were no sounds from inside the theater either.

Was there a problem with the film?

Mark pushed through the curtains to go to the projection room, but found himself face-to-face with

an ugly green tentacled creature. Thirty eyes on stalks turned toward him, and a gaping maw filled with teeth released a stench worse than the local sewage plant. Mark nearly wet himself but Tanya opened the door.

"Go back to your seat," she said to the beast.

It screeched.

"I know you're hungry, but go back to your seat. Dinner will be ready soon."

The eyestalks turned to her then to Mark then back to her. She pointed to the exit. "Go."

The beast shambled back through the curtain.

Mark let out the breath he'd been holding. "Thank you," he said.

"You owe me," she said. "You were late."

"It won't happen again. I promise. I need your signature then I'm outta here."

She took the clipboard, pulled a pen from her pocket, and signed. She handed the board to him.

"Thank you," he said, and turned to go.

Old Man Jenkins blocked his path.

"We have no tolerance for tardiness," he said.

"Please, Grandfather. It was only two minutes. I like him. He's a good guy," Tanya said.

Old Man Jenkins stared into Mark's eyes. "Yes, I suspect he's very good. Very good and very tasty to some."

"Move it, old man," Mark said, trying to push past him. The man didn't budge. He was stronger than he looked.

"You were late. There's a price to pay," Jenkins said, taking a syringe out of his pocket.

"You're crazy if you think you're feeding me to those things," Mark said, taking a step back and raising his fists.

"Grandpa, please," Tanya said. "We budgeted the time to change the film. Mark has been early some days, too. We can give him one more chance. I really like him."

"Really?"

Tanya nodded. "Let's make the one exception. Please?"

The old man hesitated, then lowered the syringe. "Mark, do you like Tanya?"

"Uh... yeah... she's... amazing?"

"Are you willing to marry her? Help her with the family business? Give her healthy children to take us into the future so I can retire?"

Mark turned to look at Tanya, thinking things couldn't get any stranger. A shotgun wedding proposal in a theater filled with freaky creatures? This couldn't be real, but it was. At least Tanya was beautiful. Even if he said yes, he could always back out later.

Mark nodded and lowered his fists when the old man seemed satisfied.

"I'd be happy to carry on the family tradition."

Old Man Jenkins smiled, and stabbed Mark with the syringe.

The world went hazy and Mark fell into Jenkins' arms.

Mark felt like he was rolling downhill into a haunted house. Green and brown creatures occupied theater seats. Some held bottles of Louisiana hot sauce. Others ketchup and mustard. One tentacled thing clutched a packet of sweet and sour sauce.

Old Man Jenkins' voice came over the speaker. "Today, we have an extra snack before our next feature begins. And Mark, I'm really sorry about all of this. Tanya's real broken up about it, but she'll get over it in time. And you can take great pride knowing you did your part to save the world."

Mark tried to roll off the gurney, but a creature leaped on him. It was the same one he saw at the entrance. It slithered its tongue over his face, then whipped out a container of greasy butter and squirted it on Mark's forehead. Next came a couple shakes of Worcester-shire sauce, and the *pièce de résistance*, a dash of garlic salt that went right up Mark's nostrils. He felt a sneeze coming on, but the creature opened its mouth wide.

Its jaws snapped shut for Mark Lassiter's final fade out.

INVISIBLE

MARIO ACEVEDO

INVISIBLE

MARIO ACEVEDO

"**A** buck fifty a car," the girl in the ticket booth says. I pass her a dollar bill and two quarters. She makes no comment that I've come to the drive-in alone. Maybe because people do. Like those who want to see a movie by themselves and enjoy it with a smoke and a whiskey. Or undo their pants to better appreciate a titty flick. Or maybe, like me, to find that special someone.

My Ford Galaxie creaks past the booth. I steer onto the field, illuminated by the flickering wash from the gigantic screen at the far end. Parked cars are scattered throughout the stumpy forest of speaker poles. I pick a spot toward the back, at the far right, and watch. Not the screen, but the cars and the people in them.

The spring night air is cool, but comfortable. I roll my window down, leaving just enough glass to hook the speaker. After lowering the volume to a buzz, I light a Pall Mall, and wait, a spider on its web. I whisper to myself. *Esta noche. Esta noche.*

My throat dries from the growing tension, becoming so parched that the cigarette smoke burns. I pop a can of Pepsi and sip, soothing my throat. I resume puffing and settle into a rhythm. Puff. Sip. Feel the refreshing coolness. Puff. Sip. Keep watching.

It's been eleven months since the last time. I've prepared myself for tonight by arranging *mis ruquitas* on the coffee table. Youthful faces forever captured in Polaroid squares. Eight girls. Ten photos of each. Too many to display at one time. I choose my favorite three from each set, arrange them in neat columns on my coffee table, and tell them: *Soon you'll have company. Chica número nueve.*

Usually, when I bring the girls out, I keep lotion and a towel handy and take my time to relive each moment of our one and only date. But earlier tonight I brought out the girls solely to whet my appetite, to sharpen my nerves for that new special someone. I propped them on my bureau so they could watch me get ready. We had a nice conversation.

The double feature is *Mortuary* and *The Slumber Party Massacre*. Girls dig horror flicks, and yet they act so surprised when I show up.

Halfway through the first movie, it's time to take a closer look at the pickings. I've pulled the bulb from my dome light so I can slip unnoticed from my Ford. I creep to the fence and check out what's going on in the other cars. I zoom in on heads silhouetted by the movie screen and haloed from the glow of cigarettes or joints. What most draws my attention is what's going on behind the steamed-up windows.

I light a cigarette. It's a way to hide in plain sight. People don't bother asking what I'm doing because the

answer is obvious. I'm some *vato* enjoying a smoke. Forgettable. Invisible.

The minutes pass. The expectation builds. *Tonight. Tonight.*

There's a ritual to my home Polaroid *fiestas*. I shower first to wash off the workday's funk. Shave. Comb my hair to a neat part. Dress in clean clothes. Shine my shoes. Gotta look good for the *chicas*. Set the bottle of lotion on the top left corner of the table.

Too bad there's no incense called *Fear*. I'd buy it if they got the smell right. Mostly sweaty hair mixed with perfume, shampoo, and a savory blend of pheromones you can't get anywhere else. Add the coppery fragrance of blood.

I study the photos on the table, eight columns, three photos each. At the top of every column is my favorite from each set; the girl staring right at the camera, our mutual gazes locked forever. The eyes are wide, the mouth distorted by a gag of electrical tape; each portrait a delicious study of helplessness and horror pegged past the red line.

I pump lotion into the palm of my right hand and begin the party. *Hola, mis queridas. Vamos a bailar.*

Intermission. Dome lamps light up. People exit cars to begin the trek to the snack bar. I toss my cigarette against the fence and join the pilgrimage. I take a roundabout path, wandering between cars, passing through clouds of burning tobacco and weed. *Cholos* stand close behind their *ranflas*, acting as if no one could possibly tell that they're pissing the beer they've snuck in. I fall in step behind long-legged teenage girls strolling in pairs, gossiping, oblivious to me.

I stand by the water fountain between the men's and ladies' restrooms, where I loiter, smoking, minding my own business while I check out the menu. I catalog the women as they emerge from the restroom. Sometimes their boyfriends are waiting. Sometimes they detour into the snack bar before returning to their cars.

It's got to be the right woman, one who reeks of recent sex. Usually in her late teens. They come to the drive-in for the privacy they can't get at home or in the dorm.

Then tonight's girl emerges.

She steps from the women's restroom, pivots at the water fountain. Holds her hair back as she bends over to drink. Firm, round *nalgas* fill her shorts. Long legs. Nice calves. Trim ankles flowing into white sneakers.

Standing, she turns in my direction. Prepared for this, I make sure I'm not looking at her when she does. The goo-goo eyes will come later.

I light another cigarette, doing my best to ignore her just as the world ignores me. She crosses her arms and walks briskly past, leaving in her wake an eddy of

perfumed soap. Much like the photos I'll take later, I record her details in mental snapshots: Slender, pretty face. Long, straight hair. *Una morena.* A local *Mexicana*? Italian? Slender frame. Five five. Hundred and ten pounds, give or take. A patterned halter top.

I count three beats before grinding my cigarette beneath my shoe and making tracks after her. I angle to the left two cars to hide the fact that I'm on her trail.

Reaching a Pontiac Bonneville, she opens the front passenger door and glides in. The dome light shines on her date. A big guy. Ruddy face. Light-colored hair. So she likes *gabachos.* No big deal. I'm not the jealous type.

I stroll past the Bonneville, memorize the license plate, but don't dare so much as glance inside. I wonder about the guy with her. In every previous case but one, it was a boyfriend. The one exception was a husband, newlyweds. I made him watch.

He had answered the door, all helpful and naive. One blow from a ball-peen hammer left him cross-eyed and stupid-faced. Then I told her I'd break his skull and splatter his brains if she didn't cooperate. *You'll both live if you do what I say.* Suckers.

Together we rolled him in a rug like a burrito, which gave him a worm's eye view of the proceedings. Technically, he made for victim number six but being a guy, he doesn't count.

Thanks to me, in the past seven years, several young women along the Front Range—Longmont to Denver to Colorado Springs—have been found murdered. The newspapers don't relate how they were killed or the exact number, but I know.

There's no mention of a serial killer prowling the area, and certainly no mention of a homicidal psychopath selecting his victims at the drive-in. Stupid cops don't have a clue. They'll never catch me because none of those strait-laced bastards thinks like me.

I fancy myself another Jack the Ripper. Too bad my name isn't Juan. That would be rich, Juan the Ripper.

I return to my car and discover I have a line of sight to the Bonneville. I spend the rest of the evening watching, calculating, getting hard. I chain-smoke, walking through the steps. We all have a calling in life; this is mine.

What makes this so satisfying are the preparations. It's a jigsaw puzzle of a thousand pieces. Years ago, I read in the newspapers how the cops caught a killer through his shoes, matching the size and pattern of the prints he'd left at the scene to the tennies in his closet. Keeping that detail in mind, I buy shoes from thrift stores, tens I slip over my eight-and-a-half size feet. I wear kitchen gloves and buy my tools at the flea market. Afterwards, the gloves, the shoes, any clothes

spotted with blood, and the implements of the night get trashed right away.

As the credits for the second movie scroll up the screen, cars start. Popcorn, wrappers, and empty cups and cans spill out open windows and litter the ground. I wait until the Bonneville moves before I crank my engine. I keep one car between us as we file out. Once outside the fence, headlights flash on. At the traffic light onto Kipling, the Bonneville heads south. I drift back several car lengths. As long as I don't tailgate, no one suspects being followed.

The Bonneville turns left at Alameda and cruises for a stretch, takes a right, then a left. I follow them into a neighborhood of older homes, small stucco boxes surrounded by hedges, roses, and sagging chain-link fences. The Bonneville pulls up to a house midway down the block.

I can't stop without drawing attention to myself so I pass, continue for two blocks and loop back, dousing my lights once the Bonneville comes into view. I coast to a halt along the curb, nerves crackling. As I settle in, another car appears in my rearview. I scooch low in my seat to hide. The car rolls by and disappears.

I bring my attention back to the girl and her boyfriend. They linger a bit. The dome light flicks on. They exchange a quick kiss. She hustles for the house and fumbles with keys at the door. Waves at the boyfriend and, certain that she's safe, he drives off. A light in a window toward the rear of the house blinks on. Roommate? Mother? No matter. Whoever they are is just another piece in the puzzle.

When you work as a field tech with the phone company it's easy to learn a lot of things about people. I use the girl's address to find her phone number, which is listed to Josefina Huerta. The mom, I guess. The record of incoming and outgoing calls reveals a pattern that tells me when to listen in. I generate a bogus work order that gets me in their neighborhood, close enough to patch into their home phone.

Girl Number Nine is Donna. Her voice is velvety, calm, self-assured, no idea I'm listening. She mentions, casually—not realizing this particular detail is so important to me—that her mom will be gone tomorrow night and she'll be alone.

I close my eyes and try not to get lost in the possibilities.

Eighteen long hours later.

From the trunk I retrieve my date kit: clothesline, electrical tape, rubber gloves, hammer, pliers, box cutter, scissors, Polaroid, and film. I slide into the thrift store shoes and stretch the Rubbermaid gloves over my hands. Palm the hammer. Donna doesn't know it but

she's as good as dead. And between now and then, there will be a lot of tears, pain, and so much fun.

On the way home, I'm burning with joy. The road swings in and out of focus. Traffic lights leave fiery trails in my peripheral vision. I'm so disconnected from my body that I force myself to breathe.

Cars shift behind me. But I don't worry about any of them. This night was too perfect. No one saw a thing.

I detour behind a Red Barn restaurant, closed for the night, and toss my shoes, gloves, and shirt into the alley Dumpster. I fling the hammer, box cutter, and scissors down separate sewers. Then proceed home. So happy. *Vamos a celebrar!*

My home is the end unit of a one-story apartment building, identical to dozens in the city, no doubt identical to hundreds in the state. It's a good place to live if you want to stay invisible.

Once inside, I make sure the curtains are drawn before retrieving the girls from where I keep the shoebox. I arrange my collection on the coffee table, selecting the appropriate photos for the party, the way the girls most certainly selected outfits for their last dates. I imagine them slipping in and out of bras and panties. Trying on shoes. Posing in front of mirrors.

I lay the newest set beside the others and make introductions. "Girls, this is Donna." I caption her Polaroids with a Magic Marker. "Donna, meet Suzanne. This is Julie. Margaret." And so on.

In every picture, the eyes are the best part. Bulging. Heavy with tears. Staring, pleading for mercy, praying for salvation that never comes.

I select three from each so I have twenty-seven photos to entertain myself. Hands and feet bound with clothesline and turning red as apples from loss of circulation. Like the finest stereophonic recording, my memory replays every auditory detail. Every whimper. Every slap.

More details swirl through my mind, in vivid Technicolor like movies at the drive-in. Complexions blanche, eyes clench, faces wince at the first touch of the blade, the snip of the scissors.

The remembered tastes flood my mouth.

The ecstasy builds and at the last second, I cover myself with a towel.

Next day at work I can't wait for time with my girls. At the office, I'm the gnome, the nobody tech, Mr. Invisible, which is all right by me. But to my girls, *soy su mundo.*

I rush home. Bring out the lotion. A fresh towel.

I recite the love poem I composed during lunch. Then someone knocks at the kitchen door. The mood evaporates, replaced by a jab of irritation.

Hurriedly, but careful that I don't scratch the photos,

I collect them in the shoebox, which I slide under the coffee table. The knocking continues, insistent. Since my Galaxie is parked out front it's obvious I'm here.

I buckle my pants and scramble to the kitchen, slowing as I approach the door. A shadow darkens the curtain over the window. I keep my voice relaxed. "Who is it?"

"Mr. Madrid, I need your help," a woman says.

Es una pinche vieja. How did she know my name? "What do you want?"

"I'm your new neighbor. I just moved into the unit at the other end of the building." My mind draws a blank. My neighbors are as invisible to me as I am to them. Again, *how did she know my name?* She adds, "My kitchen is flooding."

Why is that my problem? "Call Contreras, the landlord."

"I have but there's no answer."

"Then call a plumber."

"Even if I do, it will take a while for him to show up. Please. I got water all over the place."

Serves you right for living in this dump.

Think. Think. "The water shut off is by the back door."

"I know but the valve is stripped. I need pliers. Could you please help me out?"

Pliers. Yeah, I have a lot of pliers. And hammers. Clothesline. Tasty thoughts come to mind but I shove them aside. I need to get rid of this pesky woman and get back to my girls.

"Hold on." I release the deadbolt, then the chain lock. The instant the door swings towards me, a black shoe stomps over the threshold, wedging the door open.

A la madre! "What the hell are you doing? I said I'll help."

I should've kicked the shoe back and slammed the door. *Pero como un pendejo*, I lean into the crack to see who it is. A blond Amazon in a dark blue pantsuit glowers at me. Eyes focused like a dog on the hunt. She shoulder checks the door with amazing strength. The impact catches me off guard and I stumble backwards. She advances into the kitchen.

"Que chingados!" My vision goes red with rage and I tense to lunge at her.

Then I freeze.

Tight at her waist, a snub-nose revolver points, the copper bullets gleaming in the cylinder. I hate guns.

Keeping the revolver trained on me, she closes the door behind her. In her other hand she clasps a paper bag, hefty with bulky items.

My nerves shrink, collapsing with the realization that something very wrong has landed on top of me. I whisper, "Who are you?"

With the pinky of her gun hand, she lifts the hem of her blazer to reveal a police badge. "Detective Meredith Wheeler."

I go hollow and for a moment feel like I'm dissolving. My mind thrashes, goes vacant, and the only thing I manage to say is, "I didn't know they had female detectives."

"I'm the first on the force. Lucky you." She sets the paper bag on the kitchen table. "Get on the floor, back against the radiator."

"What for?"

She steps forward. "Don't give me shit."

"Like hell. I know my rights."

Wham!

Stinging pain explodes through my head. My vision blurs and comes back into focus as I see the cop withdrawing her left hand. *Jesucristo*, her knuckles felt hard as iron. My right cheek burns and I taste blood.

"On the floor."

I do as she says.

"Scoot against the radiator. Hands behind you." A few seconds later, I'm handcuffed to the radiator, my legs splayed flat on the linoleum.

She crouches just past the reach of my feet and upends the paper bag, spilling the contents: my thrift store shoes, the rubber gloves, the paper wrappers from last night's Polaroids.

My throat cinches tight.

She says, "I followed you from the drive-in."

It's getting harder to breathe.

"You were due," she said.

"I don't know what you're talking about."

"It was *you*." Wheeler lifts an eyebrow. "The electrical tape. Always wound in the same pattern. The same knots in the clothesline." She recites in detail the ligature marks, the bruises, the stab wounds. The size and weight of every morsel I'd left on the floor uneaten. "The same manner of injuries. Broken fingers. Blade incisions." She glances to the shoes. "Even the same size tens."

"You're crazy."

Her eyes sparkle. "After your second victim I knew there was a serial killer."

Impossible! "The newspapers—"

She snorts. "You won't get far in life believing what's printed in any newspaper." With her finger, she draws a line in the air as she explains. "I constructed a timeline of each victim's last days and hours. What they all had in common was that they had recently been to a drive-in. All I had to do was wait for you to crawl out from under your rock. Watch the calendar and—"

When she says *Bingo!* my heart about stops.

She stands and looks down at me. "I figured the West Drive-in. Why? Because you established a pattern. You boxed yourself in. At the drive-in you were easy to spot. Tucked along the fence. Watching. Smoking."

Wheeler grins, smug like she can read my mind. "No one suspects they're being followed. Especially those who think they're invisible. So that's how I caught you. You and I think alike."

I can't believe I'm hearing this. No one thinks like me.

She saunters out of the kitchen. From this angle I can't see what she is doing. My heart thumps. My nerves zing in panic. *Must escape!* I strain against the handcuffs until the cold steel bites through my skin. I give up, my heart pounding even harder.

Wheeler returns, the shoebox cradled under one arm.

Mis chicas! Though dead and silent, they can still testify against me. Their voices sing in chorus. *You are doomed.*

Wheeler drags a kitchen chair close and sits. Expression relaxed, she reaches into the box and shuffles through the Polaroids like a deck of cards.

Don't scratch them! Don't smudge them!

"I'm impressed. You do good work. Looks like you had a great time." She waves a photo of Catherine. "It's the chair for you, Mr. Elias Madrid. *Bzzzt!* Extra crispy."

My mind bolts down a hole.

What she says next draws me out. "But not tonight—"

I clutch at her words. "What about tonight?"

Wheeler places the box on the floor, then gets up and returns to the door. She opens it and retrieves something she'd left outside. It's a suitcase and a camera tripod. What the hell is she up to?

I watch her set the tripod next to the chair, then open the suitcase to remove a small portable TV, an

RCA Playmate, which she places on the chair. As she arranges things I strain again against the handcuffs, convincing myself that I would even break my wrist if that guaranteed my escape. But all I get is pain.

When I give up, I look back at Wheeler, sweat stinging my eyes. She's clamped a Sony Betamovie camcorder to the tripod and aimed the lens at me.

"You want something," I ask, pleading. "What?"

She turns toward me, presenting a smile I recognize because I've worn it myself many times. "You know exactly what I want."

My nerves zing with panic. She crouches beside me and pulls a roll of electrical tape from her blazer pocket. "I use your same technique." She pulls loose a length of tape and leans close to my face. I clamp my mouth shut. She shifts weight and plants a knee right into my crotch.

Pain jolts through me and I can't help but scream.

Wheeler is ready. She stretches the tape across my open mouth and wraps it round and round my head. Saliva pools in my mouth and I try to curse but only end up coughing spit.

She returns to the tripod and connects the Sony to the TV and plugs them both to the closest wall outlet. Gray fuzz fills the screen of the Playmate. From the case she plucks a Betamax cassette, one of several, which she inserts into the camcorder. The Betamovie clicks and hums. A grainy color image appears on the screen of the TV. A man about my age. Ragged brown hair, face red and sweaty, electrical tape gagging him. He's wearing a tank top and it appears that his arms are restrained behind him, but I can't tell if he's standing or on the

floor like me. He stares so wide-eyed into the camera that his eyeballs seem ready to pop.

A woman, who I'm sure is the detective, enters the scene, back to the camera. When she retreats, the man smacks his head against the wall and writhes as if in great agony.

His shrieks claw at my ears. Wheeler adjusts the volume until his tortured squeals are a murmur she can talk over in a calm voice. "If you ever wondered what 250 cc's of diazinon does when injected into a human body, now you know."

Blood thumps with such force in my temples that my vision goes red and blurry. Wheeler turns into a dark silhouette.

"I could turn you in, but what would be the fun in that? You wouldn't suffer, not in the same way your victims suffered." Wheeler stops the Betamovie, removes the cassette, then replaces it with a fresh one. "For the record, you weren't the only serial killer on my beat." She starts the camcorder. I see myself on the TV. "And after tonight, there will be only one serial killer left. Guess who? I hope you like horror movies. I know I do."

SCREEN HAUNT

ORRIN GREY

SCREEN HAUNT

ORRIN GREY

"**W**hat are you afraid of?" Jeanne asks, kicking her feet on the top bunk. I'm lying underneath looking up at the springs where they sag down under her weight. My mind is racing like a game of Memory, flipping over cards to see what comes crawling when exposed to the light.

What am I afraid of? How about *everything*? Dogs and spiders and those firecrackers called jumping jacks and cancer and splinters and that story about the girl who has a spider lay eggs in her face and, while we're on the subject, earwigs and that other story about the girl with an ax-wielding maniac in her back seat and the guy in the pickup behind her keeps turning on his brights but really he's just trying to warn her and infections and going to the swimming pool this summer because everyone expects me to wear a bikini but I'm too fat so I've still got a one-piece and Mrs. Conroy at school and getting a C in algebra and and and...

Eighteen years later, I want to go back to that day and give her a different answer than whatever I say, as

I put my feet on the springs and push up, feeling her weight push me back down. I want to tell her that what I'm afraid of is her not being there. But at that age, even though I worry about everything, I don't yet know to worry about that.

What Are You Afraid Of? in big white letters up on the screen of the Galileo. I'm standing in front of the seats and behind the couches. Alex is next to me in the dark, but for just a second it feels like I'm alone. The screen expands to fill my peripheral vision, and I'm just a tiny shadow in front of those massive white letters that are burning a hole in the world.

Then the letters are gone and the screen lights up with a grainy Halloween safety video that I've salvaged and adjusted to make it look sepia-toned, like an old newspaper photo come to life, and suddenly the theater resolves back into focus around me. "Looks like it works," Alex says, and I nod and say, "Looks like."

The safety video was made in 1962—the kids all wear weird, lumpen papier mâché masks and handmade costumes. It couldn't be better. At the end, it freeze-frames on one shot that I added in for the movie, and that shot pans out to become a picture in a newspaper, resolving like a pointillist painting to dots of black and gray as the camera pulls back so you can see the headline: THREE GO MISSING ON HALLOWEEN NIGHT.

The picture—which I shot on the street where Jeanne and I used to live—is of three kids dressed in homemade Halloween costumes, their masks carefully designed by Rufus Santiago, based on drawings that I pulled from Jeanne's old notebooks. A witch, a devil, and a vampire with a bat mask over its eyes.

They're walking down the middle of a suburban street at night—trees and sidewalks and only the rumor of houses to either side of them. There's just enough of a hill that everything disappears behind the rise they're cresting as they walk toward the camera; a cheat light over the ridge to cast them all in chiaroscuro, so you can see the masks well enough to recognize them later.

The witch mask is a submarine bluish-green in color, the mouth open in an uneven smile that could as easily be a grimace, the handful of teeth candy corn yellow. There's a witch's hat built into the mask; tiny and conical, with stars around the brim.

The devil has a pencil-thin gold mustache that curls up at the sides, but not the same way on either end. The mustache seems to blend like smoke with gilded arabesques that decorate the painted eyes. The devil's smile is less uncertain than the witch's; and his teeth are sharp. The vampire mask is pale with a greenish-yellow undertone; the bat is purple with green fangs.

"Seems like it should have been a ghost or something," Devin said at the bar after we showed the work print for the first time. "Or a pumpkin and a skull?" I asked.

Devin was always full of "constructive criticism." He'd asked why I set the movie in '84, rather than today, or when I was a teenager, and I told him that it was because I didn't want to worry about cellphones, which was only a half-truth—it was also because that's when the movies I grew up watching were set. Maybe he was right about the masks, but I used the designs in the notebook, and there wasn't a ghost in there.

Except that there was, wasn't there?

Not that you can see any of that in the first shot. The image is grayscale, the newspaper dated November 1964, twenty years before the events of the movie. The masks are all washed out by the faux-grain of the film. But of course they'll be back, those three anonymous trick-or-treaters.

In the script, they're identified by their masks. The Witch, the Devil, the Bat. In reality, they're played by three girls I met in film school, even though the Devil is supposed to be a boy—Liz, Viv, and Steph, their names as short as they are. I mean, I'm not tall, and Viv still barely comes up to my shoulder. That's why they were perfect to credibly play kids, without me having to jump through the hoops that actually hiring child actors and having them shoot at night would have entailed.

There are a few kids in the movie, of course. Devin's son is in there, all tousled blonde hair, and some of the kids in the theater class that Liz teaches at the high school, wearing replicas of those cheapie Ben Cooper costumes that we all seemed to wear when we were kids. But they're only for establishing shots, mostly. I didn't want them to play the monsters.

"You were always such a happy kid," my mom says, whenever I try to tell her I have an anxiety disorder, that I'm seeing a therapist and taking blue-and-white pills and things are getting better. "What happened?" *Nothing happened*, I don't say, because she doesn't want to hear it, *won't* hear it, no matter what I do. *I was always like this; I just hid it from you.*

Which isn't entirely fair because I hid it from *everyone*, didn't I? The only person who could see through my bullshit was always Jeanne, and now she's gone, so I have to do it myself.

The night before the premiere, we stay up 'til one in the morning watching the movie through on the big screen. We've already spooled parts of it up there, but never with everything going at once. The synth loops and jangling guitars from Bat Lightning, the house lights down, the whole nine yards.

When it's over and they've pulled the masks off the trick-or-treaters to reveal the mummified faces underneath—also courtesy of Santiago—and the screen has gone black and those two words come up, I find myself caught off guard yet again, even though they've always been there, and I'm the one who put them there.

For Jeanne.

"Are you all right?" Alex asks as I push past him and out the fire exit into the alley.

"I just need some air," I say, and I hear Steph stop him as he tries to follow me out.

"It's all just a lot, y'know?" she says, her hand on his arm. I stand in the alley, the streetlights reflecting on puddles of water, and cry until I stop shaking, until my breath is coming out in puffs of steam and I've hunched my shoulders under the orange-and-black sweater and pulled the sleeves down around my hands, but I'm still too cold and I have to go back in.

Fortunately, by then, I've wiped my eyes, and it's dim enough that I don't think most of the crowd could tell even if they hadn't started celebrating at about the halfway point of the film. I pull up a stool at the bar and manage a smile at Steph that I hope says, "thank you."

"Movies don't scare me," I tell my therapist at our second or third session, when she asks me why I want to make scary movies. "They're, like, the only things that don't scare me. So, of course, I want them to."

She doesn't seem to understand—and I can't really say that I do either—but it's also about as close as I've ever come to a vision statement, and I want to write it down in case someone asks me that same question in an interview or something. Y'know, once I hit the big time.

I don't ask her for a pen and paper, though. It'll take a bunch more sessions before we get to that point.

In the original screenplay, the unmasking of the three trick-or-treaters isn't the end. In the screenplay, I describe them as looking like "mummified dolls" underneath the masks—Santiago did a pretty good job of nailing that, actually—but then I go on.

They fall to the ground but don't stay still. CLOSE UP of the dust and bones as something begins to boil out of them. A green-black smoke that's too thick to be a vapor. Like when you drop a smoke bomb into a bucket of water. A witch's brew that boils through the air in three dimensions.

PULL BACK as it rises up from their bodies and starts to take form above them. CUT TO close-ups of CANDICE and JUDIE as they watch; Argento gel on the lights. In the boiling smoke brew, two huge yellow moons appear. It doesn't become apparent that they're eyes until wall-eyed pupils roll into view. Beneath them, two rows of perfect, yellow teeth.

Naturally, the Haunt, as the screenplay eventually calls the apparition, proved not to be feasible on the budget we had to work with. And even if we had been able to afford some CGI or something, I wanted to stick with effects that could have been achieved in 1984, when the film was set. So we stopped with the trick-or-treaters themselves. "I actually think it makes the movie better," Alex says. "Simpler."

I nod, as if I agree, but really, I'm not even thinking about the movie at all. I'm thinking about the nightmare.

When you're scared of everything, you learn how to compartmentalize. That's how you get through each day.

At Jeanne's funeral we bury an empty box, so I focus on that. That empty box becomes a totem—I'm terrified it will tip off its moorings and come crashing to the ground, the lid lolling open, and that Jeanne's body will come tumbling out. In my mind's eye, her body is gray and rubbery, her joints all cut black lines, like someone was trying to make a marionette. Her mouth hangs at a grotesque angle and one eye is peeled open, staring and yellow.

"Why do you girls like to watch those scary movies?" Jeanne's mom would ask, and I never had an answer, but looking back at that funeral, I have one, finally. I can handle my fear of Jeanne's decomposing body, her face

a terrible rictus, her limbs taking on the horrible life of a mannikin—better that than my fear of the truth, of the empty box and not knowing what happened to her.

She disappeared in twenty-seven minutes and four houses. That's how long it took between when she left my place and when her mom called to say she hadn't arrived home. Twenty-seven minutes through the pools of shadow between the porch lights. That was all, but it was enough.

The night she disappeared, did I hear a voice whispering outside my room, "What are you afraid of?" Or was it just my imagination? Did I dream that green face with the rolling yellow eyes outside my window as I lay paralyzed in bed?

Halloween night—the night of the premiere—lots of people arrive at the Galileo in costume. They come dressed as clowns and slashers, zombies and characters from video games that I don't recognize.

Three people show up dressed exactly like the trick-or-treaters from the film. So much so, that I have to double-take to find Liz and Viv and Steph, but there they are, all sprawled in their street clothes on one of the couches at the front of the house that are set aside for cast and crew.

The three unknown trick-or-treaters wear long cloaks, just like they do in the film, and they each carry a plastic bucket, just like in the film—a pumpkin, a skull, and the gillman from *Creature from the Black Lagoon*. The buckets were designed by Michael Schwartz, another local who makes DIY toys and sells them online, but I don't see him in the theater to ask if he made extras for whoever these people are.

"What's up?" Alex asks me, as I stand gaping near the front of the auditorium. I jerk my head toward the three trick-or-treaters, who have taken seats at the back of the house, just below the hole where the projector will shine through.

Alex reminds me that we released the short film—*Halloween Spirit*—onto YouTube all the way back when we were raising Kickstarter funds for the feature, so they had plenty of time to work on homebrew costumes. "Be flattered," he says, brushing past me to check the mics.

Someone who is finding their seat comes up to chat with me—something about how much they loved the short and how they're looking forward to the full movie—and I force a smile onto my face and nod and try to pay attention, I do, but out of the corner of my eye I'm watching those three trick-or-treaters, noting how they don't take their masks off after they sit, don't turn their heads to chat with one another. They just stare forward, plastic buckets in their laps, and wait.

Sometime after we bury the empty box, I go over to Jeanne's house and ask her mom if I can get some

stuff that I left in her room. It's mostly a lie—there *is* some stuff of mine in there, sure, but I'm there just to sit in the space that still holds her echo because it's as close to her as I can get. I sit on the bed for as long as I think I can, eyes closed, trying to imagine her weight on the bed, and then I pick up some stuff to make my story credible.

I take back my *Batman Forever* CD and a sweater that I left wadded on her closet floor, and I also take her journal. It isn't a diary—diaries are private things that you keep in a drawer and lock with a key; decorated with little hearts and butterflies. Jeanne took her journal with her everywhere. She always had it. It isn't fancy, just a composition notebook with a speckled cover that she plastered with T.S.O.L. and Misfits stickers.

She sketched in it and wrote her thoughts down in it; roughed out song lyrics for the band that neither of us would ever start. I refrain from flipping through it in her room, but when I get back to mine, I flop down on the bed and turn the pages slowly, reverently. I'm savoring each one, knowing that I'll never get another chance to look at them for the first time, and that there will never be any more.

That's how I find the nightmare. That's what the page is labeled, up at the top, in letters that have been traced over multiple times, until they almost punch through the paper. **THE NIGHTMARE.**

Ever since I was a little kid, she writes, *I've had this dream. Not even a dream. What do they call it? A night terror. I'm wide awake, or I feel like I am, and I'm in my own bed, except that I can't move. It feels like I'm pinned down, like something incredibly heavy and soft is covering every part of me. But it doesn't hurt and I'm not smothered; I just can't move.*

My room looks just like it really looks at night, but as I lay there, I notice something. There's a shape in the corner, and it's getting bigger. No, closer. Maybe both. It has a green face and green hands and it's wearing this big, lumpy black robe, like a monk. Its eyes are huge and round, with black dots for pupils and no irises. Like a Muppet. They roll around in its head independently of one another. It's smiling, and it comes toward me and I want to scream but I can't because I can't move and it reaches out its hands toward me and it smells like graveyard dirt and then I usually wake up.

Then, obviously written later, because the pen is different: *Except it isn't really like waking up, it's like I was always awake, but the universe woke up, and so the thing is gone and I can move, but I have this feeling that, if the universe ever nods off again, it'll be back.*

At about the midpoint of the movie—when the four girls are all still alive but Pete and Shelly have both been knocked off already by the trick-or-treaters—I go out

into the lobby. At my back, the screen is showing the pink neon of Wayne's Burgers on the north side of town, the place where the kids in the movie all go to hang out and fool around. For a second I can see the glow from the screen on the carpet in front of me before the doors swing shut.

The lobby is mostly deserted. A couple sit on barstools and Conner stands behind the bar in the Halloween version of an ugly Christmas sweater decorated with bloody knives and black-eyed Shatner masks. He waves as I make my way into the ladies' room, and I wave back, but I'm digging in my purse for the bottle that has my alprazolam so I can add another to the one I dry-swallowed before the movie began.

I'm bent over the running water of the sink when the door opens behind me, letting in some other patrons that I don't immediately see. It isn't until I feel them behind me that I straighten up, and when the three masks from the film are there in the mirror I drop the pale-green pill and some part of my panicked brain registers every leg of its flight as it ricochets off the sink, off the lid of the trashcan, and disappears under one of the stalls.

I try to transition my startlement into a socially acceptable laugh, though my heart has turned into a bird beating itself to death against the cage of my ribs, and my hands have already started to shake. "Those are amazing costumes," I say, acting as though they have caught me just at the end of my ablutions and trying to make my way around them to the door.

They move to block me.

My first instinct is to reach for another alprazolam to replace the one that has flown, but I know better. Whatever they're doing—the part of my brain that I have trained to shield me from the worst of my anxiety provides an endless litany of perfectly harmless explanations—I need to get out of this situation before my panic gets any worse. Once I'm in the lobby, I'll feel safer. I can ask Conner for a drink and wash the pill down with that.

"Sorry," I say, as though their move was just one of those things that happen, as you both try to get out of one another's way and end up stepping in unison. I try to move around them again, and the Devil shifts one step to the side, between me and the door. Their masks are all totally still, and all staring straight at me.

The rationalizing part of my brain clams up. There's no longer any possibility of explaining this away. No version of what's happening now is any good.

I open my mouth, maybe to scream for Conner, though I doubt he could hear me over all the various noises of the theater, but before I can make a sound, they rush me.

They smell like burning leaves, that's the first thing I notice. They're all the same height as they are in the movie, a little shorter than me. The same height as Viv and Steph and Liz. They aren't holding their plastic

buckets, and I can feel their hands fasten on me. They're wearing gloves, but still their hands feel dry, brittle. Like scarecrow hands.

"What are you afraid of?" they all ask, their voices tripping over one another as they tumble out of the holes in their masks. It's the only line they ever have in the movie, and it's provided by Greg Agee, my sound guy, running his voice through three different filters. Their voices sound just like that.

I punch one of them, the witch, and I feel the hard crack of her mask under my knuckles. It slips loose, but I don't see what's underneath—yes I do, that moving black filth—before I am running out of the bathroom.

The lobby is empty and dark. There are no street-lights outside the front windows, no cars, but I can hear the movie soundtrack, so I go back into the auditorium.

When I left, minutes ago, the auditorium was full of people. My friends were sitting on the couches at the front, watching themselves up on the screen. Now it's empty, only dust motes dancing in the beam of the projector.

The movie is still going, but the music has died just as my forward momentum does. On the screen is a scene I don't recognize—no, that's not true, I recognize it all right, I just didn't shoot it.

That green face all folded in on itself filling the screen; those rolling moon eyes; those perfect yellow teeth. An enormous green hand comes through the screen and collides with the red carpet in a cloud of popcorn dust, dragging its knuckles like Kong.

The screen isn't torn, just bulged out a little where the hand leaves it, like a swimmer breaking the surface tension of water. The other hand is sliding out of the screen now, the face stretching the surface, those rolling eyes coming toward me as the first hand slides out of its black sleeve and fastens gigantic fingers around me. They smell like graveyard dirt.

I steadied myself on the back of one of the seats when I first realized what I was seeing, and as it lifts me up, I feel my fingertips slide off the seat back one by one. When the last one slips away, I'm gone with them.

Two words burn in the dark, white against the black. They're backward from where I am, because I realize that I am behind the screen somehow, or inside it. They burn brighter and brighter until they burn through the film—even though we shot on digital, because it was cheaper—and then they're gone and everything is gone.

From wherever I am, I can hear the theater full of people clapping, though. Clapping for my movie. Clapping for those two words. Clapping for Jeanne.

THE DEVIL'S REEL

SEAN EADS AND JOSHUA VIOLA

THE DEVIL'S REEL

SEAN EADS AND JOSHUA VIOLA

T he man Richard pointed to as we entered the foyer of First Baptist Church of Harmony wore a crisp blue suit and a black patch over his left eye. He looked to be in his early thirties. The eye patch did nothing to detract from the sharp beauty of his face. Shaking his warm, large hand, the tingle I felt wasn't a bit Christian, and I hoped my attraction wasn't too obvious, considering my husband Richard and two boys, Matthew and Gordon, stood right beside me. The three men in my life wore white shirts, black ties, and had their blonde hair in identical styles, parted on the left and held in place with three pumps of Dry Look.

"Elaine, this is Cooper, the guy at the factory I was telling you about. He's also the youth pastor here."

"Please, call me Coop. How are you liking Indiana, Elaine?"

"She likes it fine," Richard said. "Or she will, once we're settled in."

We'd moved here just two weeks ago. Richard was managing a manufacturing plant that employed half the town. I was proud of the boys for their maturity in the matter. We left Denver as soon as the school year ended, which made it hard on them. Not only were they being ripped away from their summer vacation and friends, they'd have to wait until September to make new ones. Or so I'd thought. Our church back in Denver hadn't had an active youth group beyond a few kids. First Baptist appeared to have about fifty children between the ages of twelve and fifteen. Matthew and Gordon were going to make friends fast.

But Coop was the one they talked about during the drive home. I learned he served in Vietnam and found God after being shot in the eye. Coop shared his story as an act of witnessing, and it appeared my sons absorbed every word. I listened to them relay how Coop's resentment about the injury turned him into a militant atheist, war protestor and drifter. The details astonished me, but I found the story of his renewed faith just as compelling. There was no epiphany, no chance encounter with a street preacher who opened Coop's heart to the Lord. He just let go of his anger over time. As someone who rolls their eyes at *Reader's Digest* stories of poetic coincidence and grand encounters changing lives, I found the tale of Coop's recovered faith so... *reasonable.*

I was surprised at how fast our social lives became intertwined with First Baptist. The church promoted regular picnics and get-togethers. It seemed there was never a weekend we weren't gathering at some park to eat fried chicken and potato salad as one large community. Afterwards, the older men pitched horseshoes

while Coop organized the kids into a game of baseball. Watching Coop's self-assuredness and relaxed masculinity made me feel like I was fifteen again, sitting close to the field at a high school football game to steal glances at the quarterback. It was clear the older girls had a crush on him. The boys were no less jealous of his attention, always jockeying for his approval and praise in ways they never sought from their fathers. Matthew was no different, and even Gordon, who'd never shown the least interest in sports, gave all his uncoordinated effort trying to impress his youth group leader.

The summer of outdoor church socials promised to become a fall and winter dominated by the Haliled Multiplex. Construction on it started a year before we arrived, and the *Harmony Gazette* featured breathless updates on the rise of the ten-screen movie theater. Its owner, Jacob Dorenius, promised his multiplex would attract people as far as thirty miles away, and those who drove thirty miles to see a movie were bound to stay and shop or eat.

I didn't realize the Haliled was a source of tension in the church until our last picnic in late August. I'd read about the multiplex's grand opening in a couple of weeks, and mentioned to the other wives how much I'd like to go. They looked at me like I was crazy—or profane—and I changed the subject fast, holding my tongue until the drive home.

"Can you believe them?" I said to Richard. "They act like a movie theater is a strip club or something."

From the back, Gordon said, "What's a strip club?"

"Something your mother shouldn't be talking about."

"Christ," I said. "You sound like a Moral Majority member, too."

"Half the people in the factory either attend First Baptist or have family that do. There's a lot of politics in small-town jobs. Harmony is a conservative place, Elaine."

"I hope the first movie the theater plays is *Footloose*. Maybe these people will get the hint and lighten up."

Richard grunted and that was the end of the conversation. At the church service two days later, the congregation was in an uproar over the Haliled. It turned out Mr. Dorenius reached out to Coop and the youth group pastors at other churches, as well as Boy and Girl Scout leaders, to invite the kids to a pre-opening lock-in with movies and pizza.

What a brilliant move from Dorenius, I thought. He must have understood he was building his multiplex in somewhat hostile territory, but maybe he'd underestimated the community's resistance. I certainly had as I listened to people murmur and mutter in the pews. So much uproar over going to a damn movie!

There was a special church meeting the next day to discuss the youth group's participation in the lock-in. Coop subjected himself to a barrage of inane questions and inferences that left many wondering if he was fit to guide adolescents in their *spiritual journey*. I sat there biting my tongue and shaking my head with Richard

sometimes elbowing me to keep calm. But how could I? Coop was being persecuted and I wanted to defend him.

I wanted to hold him.

Guilt overcame me and I bowed my head, hearing little of the meeting until Pastor Tommy stood up and said it was time for the congregation to vote through a show of hands. Before the vote could be called, though, a voice spoke from the back. "Might I address this lovely gathering?"

We turned our heads and saw a man walking down the aisle. He was slim, his thinning hair swept back and pomaded like some silent movie era leading man. A pencil-thin moustache helped complete the look, finalized by a vest, coat and pants ensemble that must have belonged to a tuxedo popular ages ago. His appearance provoked mutters and a bit of snickering.

Pastor Tommy said, "I don't believe I know you, sir."

"Jacob Dorenius," the man said. "Owner of the Haliled Multiplex and soon to be host—I hope—of a youth lock-in that will include the children of First Baptist."

"This meeting is for members of the church, Mr. Dorenius."

"Nevertheless I am here. Like Daniel into the lion's den."

This won a slight but good-natured laugh.

Pastor Tommy frowned a bit, but relented. "Very well. We are interested in hearing what you have to say."

"First, let me start with an apology. It was not my intent to provoke controversy when I extended my invitation to your youth group. I know films have become a cesspool of violence, a celebration of deviance and adultery. I decided to build the Haliled to combat these attitudes and show wholesome pictures. I want the youth of today to care less about the return of the Jedi, and more about the return of *Christ*."

There was brief but spontaneous applause from a few people in the audience. Dorenius smiled to acknowledge them and spoke for a few more minutes. By the time he finished, every heart was softened, and those most inclined toward hostility instead peppered Mr. Dorenius with warm questions about his background, his faith, and his calling. Dorenius witnessed about the power of cinema to further God's word, describing his tearful reactions to *The Ten Commandments* and *The Greatest Story Ever Told.*

The congregation voted—the tally wasn't close—to let the youth group attend.

The lock-in was held on Friday, September 13, a bit inauspicious date-wise but practical since school started the week before. Richard drove the boys to church, leaving them in Coop's care, then came home and settled into his chair. Without saying a word, I turned off the television, sparking a bit of confused protest. Then I dropped down on my knees in front of him and caressed his upper thighs.

"Elaine—"

"When's the last time we had the house to ourselves?"

"I'm sorry," he said. "I'm just not in the mood."

His apology was as flaccid as the rest of him. I got up to head to the bathroom. He called after me, saying he was sorry, but I didn't acknowledge him. I locked the bathroom door, ran a hot bath and added some Calgon to the water. I soaked and, after a little resistance, enjoyed a feverish fantasy of Coop.

The boys came home at 8am the next morning. Their early arrival surprised me and I put on my robe and went downstairs to find them sitting side-by-side on the couch.

"How was the lock-in?"

"It was okay," Matthew said.

"What did you see?"

"Some movie," Gordon said.

The boys shrugged. I understood their lethargy. How much could they have slept?

"Want breakfast?"

"I'm not hungry," Matthew said.

"Me either, Mom."

"Stuffed from eating pizza all night?"

There was something off-putting about the smile they gave, like they were reacting to a joke I didn't know I'd made. But I was tired and distracted, so I headed back to bed, stopping only to ask if they'd made sure to thank Mr. Dorenius and Coop for a fun night.

"Did you thank Coop for a fun night, too?" Matthew said.

"What?"

I stared at them, thinking I must have misheard Matthew the first time, but nevertheless returned to bed with a cold weight in my stomach. It had just been a fantasy, I told myself. Innocent. Everyone has them.

But I'd be more discreet even in my mind from now on.

On Sunday morning, Matthew said he was too sick to go to church, and I stayed home with him. Gordon threw an uncharacteristic fit, saying it wasn't fair, and demanding to stay home too. Not atypical behavior for a younger brother, maybe, but unusual for him.

"I thought you liked going to church," I said as the three of us ate breakfast.

"You know I hate it as much as you do," Gordon said.

"I don't hate—"

"Yeah, *right*," he said, earning a sharp rebuke from Richard, who ordered him to get ready. Gordon walked out, but when it came time to leave, we found him still in his t-shirt and shorts. He sulked like a three-year-old. I watched my husband and youngest son exchanging defiant glares. Richard's fingers tapped his belt buckle with all the anticipation of a Western gunslinger about

to draw. For a moment, Gordon seemed determined to earn a whipping. Then he laughed and sprang up off the bed, dressing with the utmost cheer.

Twenty minutes after they left, Matthew's fever broke and he seemed fine, demanding breakfast and eating it with an obnoxious smacking of his lips.

"That's disgusting," I said.

"I was just imitating the sound of the water, Mom."

I squeezed my eyes shut a moment. I had to be hallucinating.

"What did you say?"

"I said: what's the matter, Mom?"

I let out a long breath. "It's not polite to smack your lips."

"Oh," he said, nodding, and began chewing with exaggerated daintiness as he stared at me.

I let it go, just like we did with Gordon. When Richard came home, he told me the main church service was disrupted by loud laughter from the youth group's classroom. Coop even came in to apologize.

"Why were they laughing so loudly?" I asked.

"Not sure. Cooper just has a way with kids."

Richard went to his chair and prepared for a long afternoon of football. I looked around for Matthew and Gordon and found them heading out the door.

"Oh, no you don't," I said, and the boys stopped.

"What?"

"You stayed home sick from church, Matthew. That means you stay home sick *period*."

"That's bullshit!"

They opened the door. I reached over and slammed it shut.

"What did you just say?"

"Nothing."

"I know what you said."

"Then why did you ask?"

Richard came and stood beside me. "Both of you get up to your rooms right now."

"No."

Richard grabbed Matthew by his arm and pulled him forward. Matthew winced as Richard's grip tightened and I saw a flash of rage that compelled me to intervene.

"Boys," I said. "Go upstairs."

I held my breath, convinced Matthew was going to continue his disobedience and provoke Richard into doing something terrible, but he marched off to his room and Gordon followed. Their bedroom doors shut without slamming and the house became quiet.

Richard's face remained bright red.

"You okay?"

"I swear to God, my father would have gone and cut a switch," he said.

"They don't need to be whipped!"

"I don't see why not. It always straightened my ass out real fast."

"They're just acting up because they're in a new place."

"It's been three months. That's not new to a kid."

"School's starting. They've got a lot of anxiety to let out and we're safe targets."

"I'll change their minds about that real quick if they pull shit like this again."

Richard was acting a little too eager for my tastes and it bothered me so much I just walked away. I took a head full of excuses with me. The boys were having trouble adjusting; they were discovering girls; they were becoming teenagers and starting to rebel a little. Before I even reached the kitchen, though, I found each possible reason falling away like a poor mask.

Something was wrong.

Tension settled over our house. Monday morning, I watched my sons eat. The only sound was the crunch of cereal and the rustle of the newspaper, that soft domestic curtain every husband and father hides behind at breakfast. Sometimes Richard would chuckle and say something like, "Mondale's still bitching," or "How in the hell can the Giants be worse than the Braves?" But this morning he stayed silent and I began to think he was somehow seeing through the pages, scrutinizing Matthew and Gordon with the stoniest of stares.

Breakfast was almost over when Gordon farted. The noise was long, drawn-out, and not a bit accidental. Matthew snickered as the odor struck us. I gagged.

Richard threw down the paper, got up and seized Gordon out of his chair.

They went upstairs. Matthew and I stared at each other and listened to the sound of Richard's belt. As the strapping went on, Matthew giggled, concealing his mouth with just his fingertips.

"Stop it," I said, and he laughed harder. I went over and shook him. "I said stop it!"

Then I slapped him.

"It's over," Richard said, coming downstairs with a strut in his walk. "I'll be taking the boys to school today, Elaine. We're going to have a little man-to-man talk along the way."

I sprayed Lysol as soon as they left and opened the kitchen window. Not wanting to think about anything, I ran water in the sink, added detergent, and began washing the dishes. I'd used too much soap and the suds built, frothy and white. I rinsed a bowl and set it aside. What I saw next made me shriek. There was a face in the bubbles, with sunken holes for eyes and an open, oval void for a mouth.

It was Richard's face.

Wind came through the window, scooped the suds out of the sink and blew it into my eyes. I screamed, stepping back. That's when the doorbell rang, followed by an urgent knocking. Disoriented, I answered the door with bits of soap in my hair to find two police officers on the porch.

They told me there'd been an accident.

The shock of seeing Richard in the intensive care unit after first looking at my children dried my tears before I cried them. He wore a full body cast. No hint of flesh showed, even in the eye, nose and mouth holes. Looking at his head encased in plaster, I knew just what he resembled, and the crazed notion crossed my mind that perhaps the face in the soapsuds was a message from him I'd not understood.

The attending physician who'd been going over the litany of Richard's injuries finished by saying, "Do you have any questions?"

"How? How did he survive?"

"Chalk it up to the miraculous. The other car struck the driver's side. Had the collision happened a few inches down, the car might have been cut in half."

"But it wasn't a few inches down, and my boys are *fine.*"

The doctor touched my shoulder. "You should be thankful for that."

I saw the obvious confusion and concern on his face and tried to assuage it with a quick smile. "Of course, I am."

He suggested I leave for now, as Richard would be in deep sedation for hours. He pushed me out of the room even as he spoke. I didn't resist until we reached the door. I was on the verge of telling him I'd leave when I was damned well ready, but I heard Coop's voice.

"Elaine."

I turned and saw him coming up the hallway. I ran to him. Ran to him like *he* was my husband. "We heard the news at the factory. Are you okay?"

I shook my head and tears filled my eyes. "It was good of you to come."

"I had to," he said, and either the answer itself or the huskiness in his voice made me study his face. The concern I saw wasn't sentimental or weepy. I suppose when you've been to war your emotions are always harder. I trembled and cried against his chest.

"I'm scared."

"Richard's a strong guy. He's going to make it."

"That's not what I mean. There's something wrong with the boys, Coop."

A rigidity entered his body. Without explanation, he pulled me down the hallway and turned a corner. We were alone and I found his face almost bloodless.

"I know. Not just Matthew and Gordon. All of them, Elaine."

"What are you talking about?"

"Everyone who was at the lock-in."

We heard footsteps and turned to see Pastor Tommy coming, shepherding my sons just ahead of him. Neither boy looked traumatized.

"Elaine," he said, reaching out to hug me. "I can only say how sorry we all are about the accident. It's a miracle from God he's alive and the boys are fine."

I might have tuned out his platitudes even under the best of circumstances, but they just made me angry. I had to find out what Coop meant.

"Pastor Tommy," I said, squeezing his hands. "I have a favor to ask."

"Anything, Elaine."

"Would you stay with Matthew and Gordon for a little while?"

His brows furrowed. "I don't understand."

"Tonight's going to be a long one here and I need to get some things from the house."

"I want to go home too, Mom," Matthew said with a slight smile. His eyes almost seemed to sparkle. There was no way in hell I was getting into a car with either of my children until I knew what was going on.

"It might be better if they stayed close to you," Pastor Tommy said.

"*No,*" I said, trying not to shout.

Pastor Tommy looked at Coop. "You know the boys best..."

"I'm sorry, Tommy, but I have to get back to the factory."

Pastor Tommy didn't notice how Matthew and Gordon stared at me. The coldness didn't belong to them. But if not, whose was it? What glared at me from behind my children's eyes?

Pastor Tommy reluctantly agreed and Coop and I left without giving him another chance to speak. Our walk went faster and faster until we began to sprint upon reaching the exit.

"Get in," Coop said as we reached his Jeep. "We'll go to the church and I'll explain everything. We'll be safe there."

We got in. Coop turned the ignition and backed out fast and reckless. I looked at his big right hand working the stick shift and noticed the whiteness of his knuckles.

"Safe from *what,* Coop?"

"The Devil."

We reached the church, parked and entered. Coop locked the door behind us and we looked out through the large entry windows at an overcast sky that felt Godless.

"Tell me what's wrong," I said.

"Something happened when we were watching the movie on Friday. I couldn't even tell you what we watched. I have no memory of it. We were in the largest theater in the multiplex. Dorenius boasted it could hold five hundred people. He said we were going to see a movie about spiritual warfare, with better special effects than *Star Wars.* That got the kids excited, but he didn't stop there. He announced the movie would be in 3D. Then he passed out special glasses."

"I know the ones."

"No, you don't. These weren't red and blue. Both lenses were the same color, a kind of amber. I'd never seen anything like them. I can't see 3D movies with just one eye, but I humored the kids and put them on anyway. I became disoriented real fast. The air was suddenly full of floating orbs of light, red even through the yellow tint of the lenses. I thought the glasses must've been dirty, but they were clean. Then I thought

it must be because I could only look through one eye.
I took the glasses off and found nothing in the air.
Then Dorenius started the film and everyone around
me started laughing. I just heard gibberish and on the
screen all I saw was static. But the kids' attention was
riveted to the screen and they were laughing harder
and harder. It was like they were being tickled. I put the
glasses back on and looked at the screen..."

I leaned closer. "What did you see?"

"I can't remember more than impressions. Perverted
things. Corruption. I shouted that we were leaving and
tried to stand but couldn't move my body. I summoned
all my strength and managed to lurch forward but I fell
into the aisle on my back. I still had the glasses on and
I could see the orbs descending on the children. They
perched atop every head. Their light was becoming
more powerful. As this went on, I realized there was a
second orb, a silver one, coming out of each kid. They
flew toward the screen like a hail of bright snowballs
and disappeared into the film. Once they were gone, the
red orbs of light seeped into the heads of the children.
As this happened, I heard chanting from the theater
speakers."

"Chanting?"

"It sounded like Dorenius. Maybe it was Latin. I'm
not sure. At some point I must have lost consciousness.

When I came to, we were all in the lobby. Mr. Dorenius was surrounded by a cluster of boys and girls, asking them if they enjoyed the movie and food. I didn't even remember there being popcorn. But the kids were so enthusiastic, asking when there'd be another lock-in. Dorenius shook my hand and thanked me for bringing them. I played along. To be honest, I wasn't sure I trusted my memories. Sometimes flashbacks of war overwhelm me and make me zone out. I figured something about the glasses must've triggered that. We said our goodbyes, loaded into the bus and I drove everyone home."

"How did they act on the bus?"

"Total silence. It didn't bother me that much then. In hindsight, it feels eerie. By Saturday afternoon, I got two phone calls from parents asking me about the lock-in. Jill Mason's mom said her daughter was sick and wanted to know what she'd eaten. Then Billy Carmichael's grandfather asked if there'd been anything inappropriate about the movie. When I said no, he said Billy was swearing, and when confronted he claimed he was just repeating what he'd seen in the movie. I renewed my feelings that something awful happened and I failed to protect them. When Sunday came, I was relieved because they all seemed fine. And then..."

"What?"

"When it came time for the congregation to break up and go to their respective rooms, I went to the bathroom and splashed water on my face. Then I went into the classroom where the youth group meets. The children were there, standing in a circle. That's how we

always begin class when we pray. But when I went to join hands with them, I was shoved into the center of the circle. They raised their right arms. Every pointing finger felt like a gun barrel aimed at my head. Their faces were nasty, cold. 'Please stop,' I whispered, and they laughed at me. Laughed the way they did in the theater, and I put my hands over my ears and tried to hide how broken I was."

"We have to call the police, Coop."

"What the hell are we supposed to tell them?"

"We could ask them to arrest Mr. Dorenius."

I knew the suggestion was bullshit even as I said it, but what other options did we have? We couldn't spend all of our time hiding out in the church. Coop and I looked at each other, coming to the reluctant conclusion at the same time.

We set off for the Haliled Multiplex.

The vast, empty parking lot gave the multiplex the impression of long-standing vacancy and desertion quite at odds with its looming, obvious opulence. The roof curved like a cathedral dome over walls of tinted blue glass. An ostentatious neon sign mounted on the edifice spelled HALILED with the same gilt glamor as any Las Vegas casino.

No wonder so many members of First Baptist felt queasy about the theater.

"Looks closed," I said.

"Dorenius is in there."

I felt certain of it too. "What do we do? Knock?"

Coop drove around back until we found an area with dumpsters and an unmarked steel security door. He parked.

"What are you going to do?"

"Pick the lock and break in."

"You know how to do that?"

He offered a shy smile and nod. We climbed out and he reached into the back of the Jeep and pulled out a black metal toolbox. When he opened it, though, I saw nothing like the hammer and wrenches I expected. There was a gun and a knife with a curved blade and saw-tooth edge.

Coop offered it to me and I held my hands up in protest.

"I'd have no idea how to use that."

"It doesn't require an instruction manual, Elaine."

I took the knife, surprised at its lightness. Coop tucked the gun into the waistband of his pants and reached into the toolbox for something I'd not seen. It was a small leather case that fit in the palm of his hand. He unzipped it to reveal a variety of delicate metal tools that looked like something a dental hygienist would use.

We reached the security door and he began working the lock.

"Did you learn how to do this in the Army?"

"No," he said, not looking at me. "Afterwards."

"Matthew and Gordon said you witnessed to them about your life."

"Believe me, I left out a lot of stuff."

He got the door open in just a few minutes, leaving me to wonder even more about those unspoken details. Coop led us into a mechanical room. I felt surrounded by a steady hum of energy.

"There's another door up ahead," Coop said, heading for it. I held my breath as he turned the knob and pulled, expecting Dorenius—or the cops. He peeked out. Nothing.

"Where are we?"

"The hallway that leads to theaters one through five. We were in theater four. Follow me."

The theater was already dark, as if anticipating its next film. The small aisle lighting was enough to reveal the largest movie theater I'd ever seen. I couldn't imagine it ever being full, and there were still nine other screens to consider.

"I don't get it. Harmony isn't large enough to support something like this. I know the multiplex is supposed to bring in people from other places, but—"

"It will bring in others. In time, it will bring in everyone."

Dorenius' voice piped through the speaker system, making me jump. Coop drew his gun, pivoted and aimed toward the back of the theater, targeting the projectionist's booth. There was a large glass window there, but if Dorenius was behind it, I couldn't tell.

"Since you took the trouble to break in, may I interest you in a special screening?"

A light shot out from the booth. We turned to look at the images on the screen. There was no sound, and the film's grainy, colorless quality gave it the aura of being very old. Children, naked and broken and weeping, staggered toward a burning lake surrounded by large, leering demons. My hand sought and found Coop's as the footage switched to close-ups of each child's stricken face. I recognized some of them. They were the children of Harmony. Members of the youth group, sons and daughters of neighbors. They were being whipped toward the fiery lake.

The camera found Matthew and Gordon and refused to leave them. I cried as they reached the edge of the lake. A demon lifted Matthew over his head, shook him like some kind of trophy, and then threw him into the flames.

I turned and screamed, "Why are you doing this?"

The film shut off.

"God treats everyone like an extra. In Hell, everyone gets a star turn."

Coop took aim again at the projectionist's booth. "I see you, Dorenius."

The film started again, striking out from the booth in a blast of light. Coop squeezed my arm and told me not to look, but I couldn't stop myself. The film showed my boys dangling over a pit, suspended from hooks

that pierced their backs. Insects swarmed their bodies, stinging and biting.

Coop was already charging toward the booth when he fired and shattered the glass partition. The film stopped, leaving the theater in darkness. I stumbled after him with the knife held tight in my right hand. Coop reached the booth and used the gun to sweep away the remaining shards of glass before climbing into it.

"He's not here," Coop said, helping me in. He found the light switch and opened the exit. As he stepped out to search for Dorenius, I stared at the projector and the film threaded through its two reels. I'd taken the boys to see *Tron* a few years ago and was amazed at what special effects could accomplish. What I'd seen on screen must have been a similar illusion. To convince myself, I pinched the strip between my thumb and forefinger and pulled until there was enough slack to hold the frames up to the light.

What I found was no less disturbing or confusing. Instead of scenes, each frame showed only a child's face, recognizable even in extreme miniature. Where were Matthew and Gordon? I pulled the reels off the projector and began to scour through the footage. The length of film kept growing, a slick, dark and cold kudzu that spooled around my feet. I began to sob at the futility of my quest and slumped to the floor, buried in film, and wept out, "Goddamnit, where *are* they?"

"They're with the Master."

I flinched. Jacob Dorenius stood in the doorway, wearing the same attire I remembered from his visit to the church. His pencil-thin moustache and slicked hair no longer reminded me of some early movie star.

"Where's Coop?"

"Cyclops is going to join the Master the old-fashioned way. I had a bad feeling about his disability. It's never been true, you know, that the eyes are the windows to the soul. Not until now. Not until the Haliled."

He held out a hand as if he expected me to grab it.

"What have you done to my children?"

"They were never yours," he said. "All men are surrogates for the Master, and women nothing more than broodmares. You may birth the foal, but it belongs to the Master's stable."

I got to my knees, holding the endless roll of film up to him in supplication. "Please tell me what you've done to them."

He draped the film over his forearm and stroked it like a pet. "I'll find them for you now," he said, and without so much as a glance he pulled at the film until he came to two particular frames. He placed them against his right ear and grinned. "They're crying out for their mommy."

"That's...that's not true..."

He pushed the film at my face. "Listen to the despair of two souls burgled through the eyes."

I reached out a groveling hand and clasped the top of his right shoe. "If you took their souls, you can put them back."

"But that would inconvenience the new occupants!"

I stared at him dumbfounded, and Dorenius shook his head.

"Think of the Master as a realtor, and each body a piece of real estate he wishes to acquire. The very wise are glad to sell to him of their own volition, but others require eviction. The children were the first but far from the last. Tonight, after all, is the grand opening of the Haliled Multiplex. There will be *many* screenings before we close. A thousand tickets sold. A thousand new servants of the Master. But let's make it a thousand and *one.*"

He threw the film aside and he grabbed me. I groped for the knife, lost somewhere on the floor. My fingers wrapped around the handle and thrust forward. The blade cut through fabric and flesh and lodged in the femur. Dorenius screamed and fell, shrieking in an unrecognizable language as he tried to dislodge the knife.

I got up and ran. My right foot tangled in the film and took it with me, trailing behind like an endless tether. I stopped to shake myself free but couldn't disentangle myself. The film began to feel like a snake tightening around my ankle, and the thought of it made me run faster.

Maybe random chance took me into the bowels of the multiplex. Maybe it was Dorenius' Master. Hell, maybe it was God's will. I fled without thinking, trying every door along the way. One was unlocked and I escaped into a concrete corridor with a winding, descending path.

I came to a single room—a chamber. The walls were painted red and lined with symbols and writing in white. One wall held the image of a goat's head, its eyes wide, glaring and defiant. The goat was so oppressive and sinister, so dominant, that it took me several seconds to realize Coop lay slumped under the image. His eyepatch had been ripped away, revealing a scar of sewn-up flesh.

His good eye had been gouged.

I went to him trembling, certain he must be dead. But he stirred and moaned.

I tried to help him up but he was too weak. He collapsed to the floor with me beside him. He took a deep breath.

"That smell."

"What?"

"Nitrate."

I didn't know what nitrate smelled like, but I did notice an acrid odor, faint but growing. "I think it's coming off the film."

Coop's body stiffened and he came alive, looking around like he could see. "In Vietnam, demolition teams would use ammonium nitrate if they needed to improvise an explosive. Nitrates were used in film a long time ago, but it made the film dangerously flammable."

A slow clap answered Coop's remark, and Dorenius limped into view. He kept close to the wall. The knife was still lodged in his thigh.

"Who says a sightless man must also be blind?"

Dorenius had the loose film bunched and draped over his left arm, as if he'd collected it all along the way. His face glowed with sweat. The agony in his expression gave me the courage to goad him.

"Too bad your Master couldn't heal you."

"The Master knows pain is the best medicine. He's already decided on *your* prescription."

He pinched the film in one spot and shook the rest of it free to the floor. His right hand went to the knife. He never broke eye contact with me as he grimaced, working the blade loose. I heard the scraping of bone, followed by a wet, meaty unsheathing.

Dorenius made two swift cuts and the film fell away, leaving two frames in his clutches. He placed the tip of the knife to one of them.

"Whose soul gets destroyed? Matthew or Gordon?"

Coop called to me from the floor, but his voice was weak and unimportant to me. All I could see was the knife. It was as if Dorenius had Matthew and Gordon in front of him with the blade to their throats.

"*Why*?" I said, dropping to my knees, hands clasped together. Dorenius withdrew the blade—but only an inch.

"The injury you've inflicted demands revenge."

"Then take it out on me!"

He sneered at the notion. "Too much of the self-sacrificial reek. No, I will destroy one frame to punish you. To save the other, you will come with me into the theater. You will wear the glasses I give you and watch my movie. And when your soul belongs to the Master, I will splice its frame next to your surviving son's—a family reunion of sorts, and the start of a new reel."

I looked up at him through teary eyes, unable to deny him the satisfaction of seeing me sob. He did not hide his enjoyment, and the knife's edge returned to the frames.

"Say a name."

He let me crawl to his feet. His pant legs were damp with blood. We stared at each other as if locked in a contest of wills, but Dorenius had won before he started.

Then Coop's voice boomed from behind me, and courage filled my heart. A bright white light rose in the room, turning the sweat on Dorenius' face into a mirror. I saw Coop's reflection, standing, the light blazing from his ruined eyes. I dared not turn around for a direct look. Dorenius dropped the knife as a beam of radiance struck him in the chest. The force of the blast pinned him to the wall.

"I AM THE LORD THY GOD."

Dorenius shrieked and fell dead. The white light increased to a blinding intensity. I put a hand to my eyes, fighting to see. The red and white paint on the walls blistered. I imagined the goat's head blackening and flaking away. The odor of nitrate became suffocat-

ing. The film caught fire. I lunged to protect the two frames still in Dorenius' grip only to have them burst into flame. I screamed, clutching my burned fingertips to my chest.

Gone.

My boys were gone.

"Why?" I said, crying and turning toward Coop, risking blindness. "Why didn't you save them?"

No voice came from Coop's mouth. He stood impassive, his right arm out, his eyes ablaze. I shouted my question again. That's when I saw the first orb. It rose from the ashes of the melted film, followed by another. One by one they flew into Coop's eyes until only two remained. They darted in front of me. I reached out to touch them and they slipped between my fingers. But I felt my boys there. I felt their kisses on my cheek as they brushed my face. Then they, too, flew into the brightness of Coop's gaze and he fell back to the ground. The light died in his eyes and I knelt beside him, holding his shoulders.

"They're inside me," he said, touching his head. "I can hear them. They're—they're safe."

"Can you put the souls back in their bodies?"

He smiled. "Help me up, Elaine. We will find the children. It is time for all of us to go home."

ON THE ROCKS

K. NICOLE DAVIS

ON THE ROCKS

K. NICOLE DAVIS

The heat of late summer descends with the sun while a hazy full moon rises in the east. Melissa and Carter stand on copper-colored stone steps, waiting to enter Red Rocks with Ashley and Derek. The natural amphitheater is typically reserved for concerts but tonight is different—it fills with moviegoers for the final "Film on the Rocks" of the year.

Melissa made sure they got there early to get good seats but several dozen people are ahead of them in line, all carrying bags bulging with seat cushions and blankets. "Thriller" plays through hidden speakers while they wait.

"What'd you say the movie was tonight?" Ashley asks.

Carter glances at the tickets on his phone and says, "*The Howling.* It's a classic."

"For a classic, I've sure never heard of it," Melissa says.

She gasps as Carter grabs her waist and wraps an arm across her chest, pulling her against him. A low snarl purrs from his throat as he bites at her neck, harder than she expects. She gently touches the spot and her finger comes away with a tiny dot of blood. Smirking, she turns and finds his lips on her own.

"It's a werewolf classic," he says. "You'll love it."

"Great," Ashley says. "Just what I want, to watch a movie about wolves. Outside, in the mountains, in the dark. Thanks, Carter."

He grins. "You're welcome."

"Didn't we watch this once? When we were, like, in high school?" Derek asks.

"Yeah," Carter says, "with those freaky chicks who kept trying to explain how right it all really is. Like how you have to survive the bite to become a werewolf. Or how the skin bubbles during the transformation from man to wolf."

Derek chuckles, remembering.

Further up the line, a group of attractive teenagers on a double date laugh. Melissa watches one of the boys—tall and broad—spit on the stairs. His girlfriend, a blonde with a large chest, sneers as he does. Melissa can see the wet spot he leaves behind as the line crawls forward.

Derek watches them too, a dark look passing over his face as he says, "Fucking high schoolers. Always so fucking annoying and disrespectful."

"Chill, man. Not tonight," Carter says and places a hand on his shoulder.

Derek turns and looks at him for several seconds, then shakes his head to clear it.

Once through the ticket scanners, the heady scents of buttered popcorn and funnel cake draw Melissa toward the food stands.

"Have you guys eaten yet?" she asks.

"I never eat before I come to anything at Red Rocks," Derek says. "There's always this sausage place—" he pauses, searching among the food and drink until he spots it and points, "over there. They have normal brats but, like, other meats, too. I had elk last time. You want one?"

Melissa shakes her head vehemently, making Carter chuckle.

"C'mon, Derek," he says, "You know your lady's a much more adventurous eater than mine. But, honestly, these days, I'm avoiding red meat."

"Suit yourself," Derek says, taking Ashley's hand and drawing her to the bratwursts.

"I'm gonna get popcorn," Melissa says.

Carter nods and heads toward the Tex-Mex stand. "Nachos for me. And a beer. You want anything to drink?"

"Soda, please. Coke or Pepsi, you know, whatever's fine."

"Sixteen ounces of whatever, coming right up."

Waiting in the snack line, Melissa listens to the crowd. Among the general hum of voices, two women discuss the merits of permed versus crimped hair in a side high pony tail. A middle-aged couple walks by, chattering about their animosity for another couple in their party. Melissa's ears perk at a sudden burst of cackling from the same group of teens that had been ahead of them in the ticket line on the stairs. Though they're at a distance, she spots the busty one with a bare midriff touching the arm of the boy who, Melissa assumes, is the high school quarterback. The other boy—smaller and wearing glasses—is basking in the laughter at his own joke. And the second girl, less showy than the other but just as pretty, covers her mouth as she giggles. Her eyes shift nervously, seeking confirmation from the flock that they aren't drawing too much attention.

Melissa looks away, moving forward with the line. Above and below the symphony of voices and laughter, coughs and sneezes and grunts, there is a whisper of wind against stone and, she thinks, skittering feet through dirt. The earth and its quieter, endemic inhabitants fill the spaces between the milling audience and their unnatural world.

In the distance, a forlorn yowl calls but is not answered.

Melissa orders a large popcorn with extra butter. The grease glistens, coats her fingers so they're slick. She grabs a couple of napkins and turns to leave, thinks better of it, and grabs a couple more.

Reunited with Carter, Ashley, and Derek, she sees they are halfway through their meals already. Carter holds a Coke out to her and she accepts it with a quick "thanks, babe."

Derek leads them down to general admission. They're early enough to have their pick of seats and they choose

a section ten rows from the front, the screen looming large and centered before them.

It makes Melissa wary, being this close. She prefers more distance between herself and the horrors on screen. It makes them feel less real. Less imminent.

Still, they settle in, setting up their cushions and laying out blankets.

Derek peers among the stands. "You guys see where those kids ended up?"

Melissa notices two of the teens are situated behind them, looking exposed as everyone else huddles close to the dais, but doesn't say anything. The crop top girl and the football player are gone and left a puddle of blankets waiting for their return.

"Seriously, Derek. Let it go," Carter says.

"Fuck you, Carter. Someone needs to let them know they can't go around acting like assholes."

"Derek. Look at me... Not tonight. You get me?"

Derek stares at Carter but isn't able to still the tremble in his hands. He takes his seat and lets Ashley snuggle against him.

The sun disappears behind the mountains yet continues to spread fingers of light into the darkening sky. The full moon glows through wisps of cloud.

Before the show starts, a Eurythmics cover duo plays a set that ends with "Sweet Dreams (Are Made of This)."

A comedian attempts a classic Robin Williams bit from his show at The Met but doesn't measure up.

Finally, the movie begins. *"We are—repression. Repression is the father of neurosis, of self-hatred... We should never try to deny the beast, the animal within us..."*

Melissa curls her shoulder into Carter's, places her hand on his thigh over the quilt they share. He feels tense, coiled, and she thinks he must recall a scary scene coming up soon. Derek and Ashley are cuddled together under their own blanket, staying warm as the temperature drops.

In the near distance, a troop of coyotes howl to one another.

"Nice of them to contribute," Melissa whispers.

Carter kisses the top of her head but keeps his eyes on the movie. His face is oddly still.

She closes her eyes and listens for the wind and the creatures that are waking to explore the dark. Bats swoop overhead. She hears a scratching noise like padded feet and claws on dirt and rock yet, when she looks, she cannot find the source. The only difference she can see is that Derek has left, probably to use the bathroom.

A scream comes from behind her. Just one at first but more follow. The cries climb over one another in length and volume, their density compounding until they're a physical weight pressing into her ears.

The rest of the audience turns to the source of the sound, ignoring the film. There's a scuffle where Melissa saw the group of teens earlier.

An object flies into the air. It takes her a moment to realize it's the shape of a human arm.

The screams continue.

"We have to move," Carter says, his voice surprisingly steady. "Now."

He grabs her bicep, right where someone would need to grip to tear her arm out of its socket, sever its tendons, rip flesh from flesh. He pulls her up, though she wants to stay down, near the ground where she can't be seen.

Her eyes search for Ashley and Derek but they've run off already.

Melissa is moving fast but she can't keep pace with Carter. Her legs trip over blankets and half-empty bags of popcorn and her own feet. Every time she thinks she's about to go down for good, Carter pulls harder, urging her forward.

Her eyes look back. She can't help herself.

A bloody mass of shredded clothes and body parts covers the ground. The jacket of the football player, missing an arm. The blonde hair of the girl in the crop top, clinging to scraps of scalp. The disembodied glasses of the funny boy.

A hairy, bipedal creature pursues the modest girl as she sprints down the empty row.

Melissa trips over a can of beer.

"Come on!" Carter growls, pulling her up.

A few more steps and they escape the amphitheater.

Carter propels her forward, not toward the parking lot, but into the mountains. She spots a handful of others doing the same, hoping to avoid the attention the throngs of people may attract.

She doesn't know how far they ran or how they will find their way back.

Eventually, they stop. The screaming is a distant call.

Even the glow of the movie goes dark.

Carter pulls her tight against him. He doesn't say anything. They stay like this, breathing heavily, and let the darkness wrap around them.

She doesn't tell him that her gums and scalp have started to itch and assumes it's just adrenaline.

Out here, in the trees and hills, the land is quiet. Only the wind and bats overhead.

Flood lights at Red Rocks come on.

"What do we do?" Melissa asks.

Carter takes a step away and gazes down the way they'd come.

"Wait until things calm down but we'll have to go back," he says.

She nods, though she knows he isn't looking at her. Neither of them move.

Something shuffles in the brush.

It comes from behind. Mangy fur and scrabbling claws and mouth open wide.

Carter shoves her out of the way, his hand pulling at the meaty back of a massive wolf-thing. A guttural snarl lunges from Carter's throat. He flings the monster

aside and it skids on all fours, its paws scrabbling for purchase in the dirt.

Melissa screams when she sees her boyfriend's canine teeth grow longer, sharper. The flesh of his face and arms bubble as they elongate. Thick hair sprouts all over him.

The wolf-thing has steadied itself. It stands upright, growling, bestial. All teeth and claws and foaming jowls.

"Derek," Carter says in a low bark.

In the near distance, coyotes howl.

Not coyotes.

Wolves.

It builds in her stomach, rising to her chest, flooding her mouth—Melissa answers.

COMING
ATTRACTIONS

STEPHEN GRAHAM JONES

COMING ATTRACTIONS

STEPHEN GRAHAM JONES

One place this starts is with the rusty access panel in the men's restroom at the old Winchester movie theater, but we don't even know about that panel until Seth tells us in super hushed tones in his basement, his eyes flicking to each of our faces, and *Seth* doesn't even know about it until his big brother, home on surprise furlough from Panama, tells him.

Once we opened that panel, though, everything changed.

According to Seth's big brother, who Seth said looked completely different with new muscles and a buzz cut and his eyes all flinty, his cheeks drawn in like a zombie's, there used to be one of those trough urinals right there on the wall of that restroom, the kind they pour ice in for you to pee on, which I guess is a 60s thing. But once people in the 70s started wanting their own personal urinal, or didn't want splashback from the guy standing right next to them, the theater ripped out the trough and put the panel up to cover the stubbed pipes and leftover support framework that was there for the trough.

The panel was metal, painted the same as the wall, a ragged board nailed across it like a Band-Aid, and you wouldn't know it was there if it wasn't rusting around the edges, where the screws had been holding it back for the last ten or fifteen years. As for why the bank of three urinals didn't go in right there, but on the opposite wall, I bet it had something to do with the ladies' room twinned on the other side of the wall, and how the plumbing over there needs to mirror the plumbing over here. The pee trough hadn't been on the wall keeping the men's room and the ladies' apart, so its place just got paneled over. Why it was on that side of the bathroom in the first place, no clue. Maybe it was a second trough, and the first was where the urinals were now? Probably that, yeah. Nobody wants to stand in line when the movie's playing.

The panel, though.

According to Seth's big brother—and this has to sort of be where it all starts—if you could wrench that panel open, there'd be a kind of dead space back there, a narrow old hall the projectionist used to use to sneak girls up to his booth back when the Winchester was grand and huge, was one theater with a velvet curtain in front of the screen, not two with a sound-leaky wall between them and a screen only half as big as it used to be.

Once we got behind the panel, into that secret space, there would be the capped pipes from the urinal trough to step over or balance on, probably pale starv-

ing spiders and clacky-fast roaches, whatever, but, supposedly, there was room in there for four or five gutsy eighth graders to stand, hide, wait.

For what?

Like I say, the Winchester is an ancient-old theater, the seats are small, the armrests are wooden, there's even a closed-off balcony. And what are old places kind of fly traps for?

Stories.

Supposedly if you drove by it about two or three in the morning—which none of us could do yet—and you didn't look directly *at* the Winchester, just kind of kept it in the side of your eye like a dog you're not sure is mean or not, there would sometimes be light in there somewhere. A dim, flickering glow. Long after all the employees had left.

It was supposed to be the ghosts watching old movies.

We didn't believe that part, of course, figured it had to be *Galaga* or *Centipede* waiting for a quarter, or the popcorn popper caught in some sad power-on/power-off loop, or a short in the exit sign. Whatever was casting that glow, we knew it couldn't be ghosts. How we knew? Because we weren't kids anymore. We were almost in high school, after all. Practically adults.

To prove that, we were going to see what the Winchester looked like after dark, and then we were going to walk out the next morning like it had been nothing. Just another night at the theater.

So, fast-forward past the four of us, me and Seth and Janelle and Klep, going to see a movie we didn't want to see, that Tom Cruise war-movie-wheelchair one, and maybe slow down to watch Klep make his way to the aisle for a popcorn refill, then hold your gaze on his popcorn sack left behind the trash, the men's room door swinging shut behind him.

Go close on his feet shuffling in the stall, waiting for the bathroom to empty out, and then back off for him cranking that board off and attacking those rusty screws with a Phillips-head, having to retreat to the stall each time someone shuffles in.

When he's got the panel off, he drops the board in behind it then just leans it in its place, a line of darkness visible above it now because it's sitting on the ground, is no longer held up by screws.

Next is me in the theater, making important eyes to Seth and Janelle—we know the plan, don't need to say it out loud—then suddenly being there with Klep, just two innocent fourteen-year-olds standing on either side of a suspiciously askew panel in the men's room.

As soon as we're alone, and moving fast because at any moment we're not *going* to be alone, we slide the panel out and I'm the first one in, my face immediately scraping rust flakes from some long-dead sewage pipe. It gets on my lips and my traitor-tongue dabs it into my

mouth so that when Klep is there beside me, I'm spit-
ting dry little pieces of grossness into the inky darkness.

We take our pre-bent coat-hangers, hook them into
the panel's screw holes, and pull it as flush to the wall
as we can. Our shoes are squelching in whatever muck
is on the floor but we hold steady, lean back, listen
to the toilets and urinals out in the real world flush,
refill, flush, refill, one of them just running constantly,
pretty much.

Next, in a moment of silence we've both been praying for, Janelle knocks on the panel, Seth at the door,
guarding the men's room. His story is supposed to be
that his friend's sick in there, like there's only one toilet
to throw up into, but whatever, it buys us enough time.

Janelle ducks in, stands up already tying her hair
back so it won't catch in the pipes and rust and brackets
and wood all around us.

It's a double-rush for her, since this is both a secret
space *and* the men's room.

"Just two stalls?" she hisses.

"Shh," Klep tells her.

Fourteen flushes later, Seth knocks our knock on the
panel and ducks in, and, using our shoestrings because
we didn't plan on this part, we tie the back ends of the
coat hangers to the pipes all around us, so we don't have
to keep leaning back to keep the panel in place.

"I should have peed while I was in there," Klep admits to the three of us.

"Don't you dare," Janelle tells him.

Klep gulps, his eyes probably floating yellow.

Somewhere out there the movie goes over and the crowd shuffles out, at least half of them stopping by the men's room, I'm pretty sure, and then, what feels like thirty minutes later, someone out in the bathroom is...mopping?

I shush Janelle when she starts laughing for some reason, and, under cover of the slurp-slurp of the mop going back and forth, Klep tries to sneak a pee in the back corner.

I'm glad I can't see Janelle's face. Or, I guess, I'm glad she can't see mine and Seth's, each of us about to burst with laughter and give us away to whoever's on mop-duty out there.

"Sorry," Klep says when he's back, which is right when the panel shakes from a bucket rolling into it.

Of course a shoe-string knot gives.

We all dive for it, none of our fingers quite catching it...except Janelle's.

She doesn't slap the panel back into place, just eases it back in.

Out in the light, the mopping stops for a moment.

In the darkness, we're all praying hard, trading our souls for this mopper to not need the hassle of something *else* to fix in a broken-down old theater.

Our souls are, apparently, accepted.

Jump ahead to Janelle dashing across to the darkened ladies' room and Seth taking his turn at the actual urinal, me choosing the stall, as usual.

We meet in the lobby, four timid shadows, *Ms. Pac-Man* the only machine making noise.

"Still smells like popcorn," Klep says.

Seth makes a show of taking a sniff.

"So where are these ghosts, then?" Janelle asks.

"There," Seth says with a smile, nodding down to the blue ghosts running away from Ms. Pac-Man. Janelle pushes him.

"What time is it?" I ask, I guess kind of uselessly, as nobody bothers to check.

On cue, two U's of yellowy light outline the double doors, which are kind of weird already: when the theater was one huge screen, they were the back-middle doors you could kind of make a grand entrance through. Now that the theater's split into two screens—two smaller theaters, a wall between—each door opens into a different theater. The left is A, the right is B.

So, it's kind of weird already, but? Light glowing around the doors to A *and* B at the same time, that's double-freaky, can only mean that both projectors for each theater came on at the exact same time.

"Ask and you shall receive," Seth recites like an afternoon horror movie host.

Klep takes a step back, eyeing the exit doors behind us. I know he is because I am too, can see our four reflections thin in that glass.

Klep gets there a step before me, shakes the one he's at to show how locked it is. I shake mine as well, just as frustrated, my heart pounding just as hard, my mouth just as dry, my eyes hotter, I'm pretty sure. More desperate.

"In for an hour, in for the night," Janelle says, not reciting anything, just making it up, and also making her voice spookier than it really needs to be.

Seth laughs a nervous nothing-laugh.

"Shouldn't we see what's—what's playing?" he says.

Klep shakes his head no.

"I'm with him," I say, no eye contact.

Janelle is disgusted with us.

"It's okay," she says, turning to face those scary doors. "We won't tell anybody you stayed in the lobby like little babies."

Klep catches my eye and I catch his back, and, to be honest, I'm pretty fine with being a baby, if I can be an *alive* baby. It's the obvious decision.

"We're not supposed to split up though," Seth says, and he's right, this is one of the rules we established before starting this stupid caper.

"And it's not a democracy either," Janelle says, well before we can put anything to a vote.

She turns around, walking backwards into this, staring each of us down. Not so much daring us as calling us out.

Seth is the first to fall in with her. Next is Klep, stepping forward like offering his head to the guillotine, leaving me suddenly alone in this now-empty part of the lobby. Me and Ms. Pac-Man.

I picture myself standing out here by myself after the three of them have gone into either A or B.

What would happen if I looked over to the concession bar and there was some 60s soda jerk in a paper cap waiting for me to tell them I want a large…what?

I don't wait to find out, just close my eyes, stab my right foot out, then my left, delivering myself all the way into this.

The first thing wrong, and wrong in a huge impossible way, is that when we pull the double doors open, it's not into either theater A or theater B.

Spread out before us, the seats sloping down to the monstrous screen, is a single theater. The *old* Winchester.

"No way," Klep blurts out, reaching for where the dividing wall should be.

"Way," Seth says.

"Look," Janelle says, and we all do.

The screen still has this massive red-velvet curtain draped across it.

"But the movie was—" I counter.

"That was the coming attractions," Janelle says, taking a slow step into this. "The—the movie's in a different...what do they call it?"

"Color?" Seth asks.

"Panavision," I fill in, but would the curtain really close just to reset that? It doesn't matter. Janelle takes Klep's hand, Klep takes mine, and I reach over for Seth. This isn't the part we're ever going to tell anybody about.

"It's waiting for us," Klep says, and I don't know how I know this, but he's right. The movie isn't going to start until we're in our seats. The Winchester is old-fashioned and proper like that.

The four of us make our way down the aisle hand in hand, our eyes all over the theater. I'm expecting, with each new pillar or seat my eyes cross, to have just missed seeing someone—to only be seeing the motion of them stepping away, not the actual ghosts themselves.

It's just us, though. Somehow that's even worse.

"Here," Seth says, and we take the row he means, fold the seats down, let them hold us.

Just like Klep said, the curtain draws back.

"What'll it be, you think?" Janelle says.

"*Road House*..." Seth says, trying to force a chuckle but also not letting go of my hand even a little.

Road House would be good. *Road House*, *Batman*, even stupid *Little Mermaid*, or the rest of the 4th of July movie we skipped out on.

No *Pet Sematary*, though. No Freddy tonight, please, no Jason, no Michael in his white mask, with his dead eyes.

I squeeze Seth's hand when that dusty finger of light points down over our heads, finds the screen. At first the image is all blurry and hurried, but then whoever's up in the booth finds the focus, slows it down, gives the trees up there crisper trunks, sharper leaves, deeper shadows.

This isn't just random trees, either. This is the... *jungle?*

"At least it's in color," Klep says with a sort of gulp.

Green. Green is the color.

It's the color the soldiers moving through those trees are wearing too.

"War," Janelle says for all of us. "It's a war movie."

She's right.

"South America?" I say, trying to put a name on it so I won't have to be so afraid. "Panama," Seth says with enough authority that I have to look over to him to gauge his face.

He's just staring up at this happening on-screen, his mouth hanging open.

As if confirming his *Panama*, we swoop around to see a side profile of the third-behind soldier, creeping through the foliage, trying to meld with the shadows.

It's Seth's big brother.

"Dane," Seth says, leaning forward with his heart.

My scalp crawls, my head is shaking no, no, no.

"We've got to—" I say, standing, but Seth's hand holds me there, and nobody else is standing. They can't look away.

"Wait, wait," Klep says, angling his head over to see where Seth's big brother is looking: ahead through the trees, past the soldier, into—

The scope with him in its crosshairs.

The bullet catches him in the throat, and I guess because that's soft tissue or whatever, it doesn't throw him back, just goes straight through, and it's like someone pulled the plug in his neck, because all his blood is gushing out.

Now there's green in the background and bright red bubbling up through Seth's brother's fingers, his breath loud and choked through the speakers.

Seth pushes up and back, away from this, ends up sitting on the front edge of his folded-up seat, his eyes about to cry.

Mine too.

"But, but, but—" he says, and I know what he's saying: but his brother was knocking on the door just last week.

Or was he?

Or, no: *what* was he?

The screen sucks down to black, and in the slight afterglow, I look over to Janelle and Klep for support, so they can help me talk Seth down—yes, his brother is dead, yes, his brother was dead all along, but that doesn't mean we can't get up, throw a trashcan through the doors, still make it out.

I don't say anything, though.

Klep's face is leathery and caved in, and Janelle's hair is hiding most of hers, but there's a roach flicking into her eye socket—no, what I'm seeing is where a roach *just* flicked into her skull.

I push away, fall into the row, and Seth's arm comes with me, is dry, breaks off that easy.

I shake it off, push farther away toward the aisle, my shoulders and the back of my head catching on the butt of the armrests from the row in front of us.

How can this be? They can't be...they can't be dead already, can they? *Can* they?

And then the next armrest I bang into, the impact shakes a rusty screw loose.

It tings down, lands on the top of my hand. I shake it off fast like it's a maggot and it—it sticks to the back of the seat beside me?

Not just that.

It sticks and then it rolls up to the armrest it's been holding in place for the last two or three decades.

Worse, it screws back into its old hole with a small screech.

There's a version of the Winchester that never decayed, that won't fall apart.

That's where we are now.

I shake my head no, no, no, turn and run, falling twice but finally making the lobby, *not* letting myself look across the concession counter, *not* listening to all the change-flaps on the games clattering back and forth, *not* smelling any of the popcorn, just diving hard for the men's room.

The floor in there is wet but I don't care, just slide to my knees through it, my fingers coursing along the back wall, feeling for the lip of the panel.

I just manage to hook it, latch on and pull, but—

What?

"No, no no no," I say, insist, pray.

Just like the armrest screws, the screws holding the panel to its big square hole in the wall have found their old place.

The panel's tight, fast, *there*. This isn't a tunnel I can rush the other way back through. This isn't a thing I can undo. And...this *is* where it starts, isn't it? Four kids, daring each other, emboldened by a story from a dead brother, crept into a dark open space in the wall one Saturday night, and they pulled the panel shut over them, blocking the way out, and they waited there for everyone to leave, only, they're still waiting, they never left.

They're in there now.

Years down the line, during whatever renovations the 90s call for, when the panel finally falls away, there will be the four famously missing teens, mummies now, starved and leathery.

We'll be holding hands, but our real selves, they'll still be in the Winchester, watching movies we shouldn't be watching, the house lights long gone down.

LATE SLEEPERS

STEVE RASNIC TEM

LATE SLEEPERS

STEVE RASNIC TEM

T ed woke up in the dark with a dull headache, deciding to sneak out before the rest of the family got up. Going home for Thanksgiving was a terrible idea. He'd have to find some excuse to stay on campus for Christmas. Maybe he'd come home New Year's Day, if he wasn't too hungover.

He'd slept in the same clothes he wore at dinner. He didn't know why he hadn't changed; he didn't remember going to bed. His dad worked all day on their ancient furnace, banging a hammer and making dinner late. Mom was furious, and that started the first argument. Then his brother got into it, followed by his brother's wife. There'd been something about Ted's major, the wasted college fees, his low grades, and other upsets he couldn't remember at all. Politics maybe. Or a neighbor's careless and tragic end. So much he couldn't quite point to. For once his dad hadn't participated. He just sat there staring at them. Ted remembered leaving the table mad at everybody, but nothing after.

The meal might have gone better if Emily had come. They might have tried harder with a stranger present, but Emily was amazed Ted had even invited her. "We don't have that kind of relationship." His confusion and embarrassment over her answer made him feel stupid. He'd promised them his girlfriend was coming for Thanksgiving. His brother always gave him shit about his "unrequited loves."

Just once Ted wanted to be the one who got the girl. In the movies, the loser sometimes got what he wanted. That was supposed to encourage guys like him.

He carried his coat and bag out to the staircase landing. The inside of the house appeared unfocused, layered in shades of gray. He couldn't have said what about that bothered him. He strained to see more detail, making his headache worse.

He crept down the staircase gripping the railing and watching each step. He walked into the dark dining room. The table should have been empty, but he could see a spread of silhouettes. He flipped on the light. Dirty plates were still around the table, greasy glasses and silverware, a fork under his sister-in-law's chair, debris from the great bird and bits of lettuce and bread scattered across Mom's best tablecloth, a bowl almost empty of mashed potatoes, an unserved pumpkin pie. His father's plate was still full, surprisingly untouched.

His mother hadn't cleared or cleaned anything, yet she was such a neat freak. Had she been that angry? Or maybe she'd gotten sick. He'd call in a few days and apologize, make sure she was okay.

He paused at the front door. The stillness troubled

him. He didn't hear anything, but it seemed the noise of nothing was pounding in his head. He breathed in deeply, smelling only the stale air. Maybe all would be forgotten by his next visit.

No one was up in their small town. The downtown Christmas lights were hung, a glitter of brilliant white with the occasional splash of red. Everything else lay dark.

A half hour outside town, Ted saw the *Paradise Cinemas* sign, the only building visible for miles. The vertical theater name and the rectangular marquee below were outlined with a triple row of blinking blue and red bulbs. He'd gone there all the time when he was a kid. It was the first twin cinema in this part of the state. Showtimes were staggered so you could see a movie in one theater and then move to the next. By his high school years, most people had taken their business to the eight screens at the new multiplex.

The Paradise used to run movies all Thanksgiving night for those with no better way to spend the holiday. He slammed on his brakes to make the turn onto the access road, the rear end of his Celica fishtailing on the icy pavement. He felt suddenly ill. He stopped the car, opened the door, and threw up onto the road.

There were six or seven cars in the gravel parking lot. The marquee said "Late Sleepers & S*l*cted Horror Clips." A hand-lettered cardboard sign on the art deco door stated "Final Day / Thank you for 50 great years!" The theater's front door made a soft scraping noise as he stepped into the ice-cold lobby.

The interior had the same décor Ted remembered from childhood. The carpet bore a complex pattern of Asian temples and jungle animals in several colors. Badly worn when he was a kid, it was far worse now. Dark floorboards peeked through in spots. The wallpaper was pinkish-red and flocked with a felt pattern a few shades darker. The main figures resembled giant upside-down roaches. The chandelier overhead was missing numerous prisms and other glass trim.

A huge man in a pale-yellow suit and a fur cap stood up from a chair wedged behind the heavily-scratched glass counter. His forced smile looked painful. His "Manager" tag was pinned to a ratty-looking red sweater beneath his suit jacket. "Hello sir, welcome to Paradise," he uttered in a monotone. His lips were wet and his eyes red and tiny.

"Hi, the movies still playing?"

"Right until dawn."

"How much?"

The manager pouted. "Usually five bucks, but this is the last night. Let's call it free. Besides, the main feature, *Late Sleepers*, is a weird independent film out of Atlanta. But it's all we got."

"I can't argue with free. What are the clips on the marquee all about?"

"Just a bunch of scenes the owner put together from stuff that's played here. I don't know where he got it all. Some of it he's had for years. Sometimes a reel falls apart on you, you know? Sometimes part of that reel doesn't get put back." It sounded dubious, but what did he care? "Can I sell you some refreshments?"

"A medium Coke, I guess."

"Popcorn? Candy?"

Ted looked at the popcorn maker, half full of yellowish, stiff-looking popped kernels. The butter appeared discolored. The candy bars sat neatly arranged in the glass case but they all had faded wrappers. As he surveyed the offerings, he was pretty sure most hadn't been made in years—*Marathon, Reggie, Starbar, PowerHouse,* and *Texan.*

The manager had the drink ready on the counter, two thick fingers tapping the lid. "The Coke will be enough. It's kind of late," Ted said.

"Three bucks then. Find yourself a seat in theater two. Movie's on a loop. You're about forty-five minutes from the end before it all starts up again. Stay as long as you like, until dawn at least. That's when I kick everybody out and the Paradise is done. Next month they're turning us into a parking lot." He made a hoarse, gurgling laugh.

Ted had no idea what he was talking about. "What's playing in theater one?"

"We shut that one down years ago. Projector went bad. Couldn't afford to replace it. I like them old projectors. They make a little rattling noise that tells you you're in a theater and not watching TV."

Ted nodded and walked to the gold curtain with the black numeral "2" above it. A small paper sign by the opening said *No Sleeping Allowed*. "Are you serious about 'no sleeping'?"

"I am. People snore—it disturbs the other customers. Almost worse than talking."

"But people fall asleep during movies all the time."

"Not in my movie theater. They get one warning. After that, they're gone."

"I see..." Ted paused. The manager's face became angry. "I've never heard of this before."

"It's like church. You're not supposed to sleep in church. You let the screen do your dreaming—that's what it's there for. Did you know in the 30s they called movie theaters dream palaces? They understood back then. We've just forgotten."

"Well, thank you. I didn't know." Ted pushed apart the curtain and stood inside until his eyes adjusted. He hoped he wouldn't fall asleep. It was pretty late.

More of the old carpet ran down the aisle. The rows of seats looked uneven as some seat backs had collapsed and some were missing corners. He could see very little of the walls in the dark, but he remembered huge water stains descending in some sections, and even bigger ones flowering across the ceiling. He doubted they had been fixed.

The screen was watchable, despite several vertical splits and puckers near the edges that distorted the image. It was framed by two halves of a giant red velvet curtain. He wondered if they still closed the curtain between shows. Even in its shabby state it suggested the possibility of something grand.

His tennis shoes stuck to the carpet with each step, making a soft kissing noise when he lifted his feet. All those decades of dripping butter and pop, he thought. He looked for the seats that appeared less worn, less sunken. Pickings were slim. He tried several before finding one somewhat bearable. He had to squeeze past a few patrons as collapsed-looking as the upholstery. His apologies were met with silence.

He assumed the scene playing on the screen was from *Late Sleepers*, but he couldn't figure out what was going on. He was looking at a vaguely familiar living room in a modest home somewhat like his parents', so dark it might have been black and white but for a few visible glimmers of blue and green. The soundtrack had a discordant metallic hum, the rhythm of which shifted unexpectedly, increasing in volume gradually until he found himself wiggling around in discomfort.

The scene went on with no actors, and no other sound except for that loud mechanical noise. Ted began to wonder if there might be something wrong with the projector. He twisted around and checked out the rest of the audience, looking for impatience or confusion or alarm, anything indicating they might be seeing it the same way he was.

There were eight or nine forms slumped into their seats, heads tilted back, motionless. Ted couldn't see any of their eyes, but from their attitude and their still- ness, it seemed some of them must have been asleep. Maybe all of them. They were breaking the special rule of the Paradise, so why hadn't they been removed? They were completely silent—no snoring that he could hear. He couldn't even hear them breathe. Perhaps making noise was the major concern.

He returned his attention to the screen just as the machine noise faded and the scene ended. The words "End of Part 4" appeared.

There was some scratchy black leader and then the first clip began, or at least the first clip Ted had seen. A hand-written title appeared in black ink over white stock. *Possession*. He'd seen it, if it was the one he was thinking of. Isabelle Adjani appeared walking through a heavily shadowed subway passage and he knew immediately it was that movie. Suddenly she was convulsing, throwing herself around as if an outside force controlled her body. Ted clutched the armrests, knowing what was coming. Isabelle fell to the dirty pavement in agony, hemorrhaging copiously as she had a miscarriage. They'd picked the most terrible scene from the film.

The "clips" appeared to be a compilation of scenes from 70s and 80s horror flicks, many Ted recognized

and many more he did not. They ran without inter-ruption, separated only by dark or bloody or plain nasty-looking leaders, each introduced with a hasti-ly-scrawled identifying title, one after the other like a feverish, disjointed nightmare.

Next came Jason's rotting body pulling the girl under the lake in *Friday the 13th*. Then there was Chucky coming alive in the mother's hands in *Child's Play*, followed by an illegibly-labeled clip in which a baby ate its own fingers in a jittering black and white soundless sequence so badly scratched Ted wondered if maybe he just imagined it.

The music behind many of the scenes was loud to the point of distortion, the colors so bright and garish they appeared to burn through the screen. His head ached again. Then came that awful ending to *Sleep-away Camp* in all its politically incorrect glory, the shattered looking face he had never been able to get out of his head. Ted felt ill again so he climbed out of his seat and ran for the bathroom off the lobby.

The manager wasn't behind the counter. The men's room was under the staircase leading to the closed balcony. As far back as Ted could remember, the balcony had always been closed. He squeezed through the narrow doorway and down a crooked hall. At some point the three toilets and sinks had been painted bright red, but the paint was mostly chipped off, leaving a haphazard blood-spatter effect. He went to his knees before the first bowl and vomited, almost passing out. He put his head against the cold floor, vaguely aware of how filthy it was. He got his head above the bowl before vomiting again.

He had no idea how long he was in there, and he felt no urgency to return to his seat. He rubbed water onto his face and into his hair and staggered out. Still no sign of the manager.

As he walked past theater one, he thought he heard a noise from inside. Like the sound of a projector motor. He pulled the curtain back and peered inside. The projector clattered above his head. A bright white nothingness flickered on the screen. The dark outlines of all the seats appeared swollen and misshapen, as if occupied by a sold-out audience. Suddenly a heavy hand on his shoulder pulled him back into the lobby.

"I told you that theater *ain't* open to the public!" The manager's face was livid and dangerously close. That hadn't exactly been what he'd told him but Ted wasn't about to argue.

"I'm sorry. It won't happen again." Startled, he squirmed away from the manager and ducked back into theater two. He felt sick with embarrassment, like some stupid kid.

Late Sleepers was apparently in the midst of another chapter. Still no actors in evidence, but the camera was taking the audience up a staircase and down a hall, presumably to the bedrooms. The hall was so dark Ted could make out very few details. It all looked terribly

familiar, but then many houses built during that time had similar layouts. Then "End of Part 7" flashed on the screen. He had no idea he'd been gone that long. There seemed little point in staying—he hadn't seen any characters yet and had no idea of the plot—but another round of clips began and he was reluctant to leave.

Several odd characters scrolled across the screen, followed by some quick cuts of an old lady being ripped apart by giant demonic crickets in some nameless, sickeningly-lit Asian film. This was followed by the exploding head scene in *Scanners*. Apparently, the owner, who Ted strongly suspected was also the manager, liked this so much he repeated it twice.

After a pause and random streams of color, he was treated to the incredibly visceral transformation scene Rick Baker delivered in *An American Werewolf in London*, one of Ted's favorites. A couple of friends once claimed it was a comedy but he couldn't remember ever laughing.

The next clip began but almost immediately bubbled and burned. The house lights came up abruptly and Ted could hear cursing—or was it screaming?—coming from the projection booth behind him. He saw an irregular patch of shadow flowing down the center aisle and realized it was a mass of roaches fleeing the light. They disappeared into a rip in the carpet. He turned around wondering if anyone else caught a glimpse. Some people must have left because now he could only count four besides himself. Three of them had their eyes closed, heads tilted sideways. The remaining pallid elderly man stared at him, unblinking. He slowly caressed the curved handle of a thick wooden cane he had clutched to his chest. Ted turned away.

It was his first chance to get a good look at the theater's walls and ceiling. The stains were still there, but multiplied. In some places, the wallpaper had disintegrated completely to show separating sections of plaster, their edges gleaming with moisture.

The lights went out again and the clips continued to roll. The tree outside the boy's window in *Poltergeist* warped into footage of the overactive hand in *Evil Dead 2*. The clip ended abruptly and went directly into Jeff Goldblum's final transformation in *The Fly*.

The deep suggestion of filth in that movie made Ted feel profoundly uncomfortable. He shouldn't have left his parents' house so abruptly. He should have stayed and made amends, helped them clean up the dreadful mess the next morning.

The nasty kitchen in Tobe Hooper's *Texas Chainsaw Massacre* appeared on the screen. It was an unstable clip, which only fueled the electric anxiety of the characters. Layers of flesh and bone debris, greasy plates and silverware, dried regions of blood. Ted began to sweat, and a burning sensation moved across his chest. He wanted to scratch himself, but the itch spread everywhere, and once he started scratching, he couldn't imagine stopping. Things moved in the far corners of

the scene, a suggestion of insects wandering across the table and touching the scattered bits of food, something crawling in and out of a small carcass, a suggestion of a rodent.

"End of Part 3" flashed on the screen, followed by some scratchy leader, then more footage from *Late Sleepers*. The pieces must have been out of order, not that it mattered as far as he could tell. Still no actors. The camera moved slowly into the dark dining room when a small spotlight, like a flashlight—presumably attached to the camera—went on and off to illuminate individual plates, serving platters, wine glasses tipped over and staining the lovely tablecloth with splotches of deep red. Grease gleamed off the fine holiday china and close-ups zeroed in on forks, knives, and spoons smeared with animal and vegetable remains.

Ted grew increasingly anxious as each new detail was revealed. With the camera so close to the table this could have been anyone's dining room, and holiday meals had a certain uniformity across the country, but some angles and perspectives appearing at such size across the theater screen shook him with unsettling recognition. The burning and itching returned and were more intense, like armies of filthy insects marching around his torso. Soon it was almost unbearable. He jumped out of his seat again and raced for the bathroom.

Once under the mirror's bare bulbs, Ted shed his coat and peeled off his shirt and stared at himself. Large cherry-red blotches covered his pecs and belly. Even brighter red islands had risen on his forearms, like the flocked patterns of the lobby wallpaper. These continued onto his hands, blistering one of his knuckles. He probed the tender spots, searching every inch of skin to map the spread of his symptoms.

Maybe he was allergic to something on the seats, and the blotches would be gone by the time he got to campus. But this place was so filthy, it could be anything. God, he should never have drunk that Coke! It was probably contaminated. He might have to go to the infirmary once he was back on campus. Not that they could help him. He wondered if they were even real doctors. He locked eyes with his mirror image. It was like watching a movie of himself. This damn Thanksgiving. His damn family. He'd heard that sometimes people got rashes just from being upset. Well, he was plenty upset. Every time he came home he was upset. He should have left right then, but he wanted to see how it all ended. He put his clothes back on and went into the lobby.

The manager had the elderly man Ted saw earlier in theater two trapped in his arms, dragging him away. The old man's cane fell to the floor. The manager glanced at Ted and growled just as the man went slack. "*Go back to your seat!*" the manager barked as he hauled the poor man into theater one. Ted could hear that projector clacking and whirring so loudly, it must have been flying apart.

He wanted to help the fellow, and started after them, then stopped. This wasn't a movie, and he was no match for a behemoth like the manager. He went to the front door and struggled to open it. It was locked. He looked around frantically, expecting the manager to burst through the curtains. A payphone hung from the wall by the restroom door, but the handset had been removed, colored wires splaying from the armored cable. He picked up the cane, and ran back into theater two looking for help.

Ted scanned the seats. The theater was completely empty. A snippet from John Carpenter's *The Thing* was playing—that hideous upside-down head growing segmented legs and trucking rapidly across the floor.

He ran to the front of the theater and used the cane to pull back the curtains on both sides of the screen. The two emergency exits were boarded up. He walked back up the aisle trying to figure out what to do. He avoided touching the seats. He turned and gazed at the screen.

"*Heeeeere's Johnny!*" as Jack Nicholson's head protruded from a jagged hole in *The Shining*.

Late Sleepers started playing again. The camera glided along the upstairs hall of that too-familiar home. Ted needed to leave, but there appeared to be nowhere to go. He gripped the cane tightly, getting ready to use it as a club. Up on the screen of his dream palace an unseen hand opened each door along the hallway and the camera, and Ted, floated inside. In the first bedroom his parents lay on the floor, dead eyes staring at the ceiling, their cheeks bright red. In another room the bodies of his brother and sister-in-law lay contorted in bed, tangled in the covers. The rising sun peeked through the window.

The film ended, fading to black before it got to Ted's room. He ran out to the lobby, cane raised. The manager was nowhere to be seen. Ted waited, looking around, listening carefully, hearing no sound. Then he noticed that the front door was cracked an inch or so, just enough to let in the dawn. He slammed it open with his shoulder, turning and swinging at nothing until convinced he was alone.

Ted drove back to his parents' house, understanding he would not be returning to school, a surrender more than a decision. The filth and chaos of the dining room looked worse in the light of morning. He thought back to the beginning of that terrible day, and how it all seemed to begin with his father's frustrations with the furnace. He breathed in deeply, seeking some kind of smell, but there wasn't one. He quietly climbed the stairs even though he knew he risked disturbing no one. He thought about peeking into the other bedrooms but didn't have the heart. He took off his shoes and climbed into bed with his clothes on. He might have taken the time to slip into pajamas, but he knew it wouldn't be that kind of sleep.

SPECIAL MAKEUP

KEVIN J. ANDERSON

SPECIAL MAKEUP

KEVIN J. ANDERSON

T he second camera operator ran to fetch the clapboard. Someone else called out, "Quiet on the set! Hey everybody, shut up!" Three of the extras coughed at the same time.

"*Wolfman in Casablanca*, Scene Twenty-three. Are we ready for Scene Twenty-three?" The second camera operator held the clapboard ready.

"Ahem." The director, Rino Derwell, puffed on his cigarette. "I'd like to start today's shooting sometime *today*! Is that too much to ask? Where the hell is Lance?"

The boom man swiveled his microphone around; the extras on the nightclub set fidgeted in their places. The cameraman slurped a cold cup of coffee, making a noise like a vacuum cleaner in a bathtub.

"Um, Lance is still, um, getting his makeup on," the script supervisor said.

"Christ! Can somebody find me a way to shoot this picture without the star? He was supposed to be done half an hour ago. Go tell Zoltan to hurry up—this is a horror movie, not the Mona Lisa." Derwell mumbled how glad he was that the gypsy makeup man would be leaving in a day or two, and they could get someone else who didn't consider himself such a perfectionist. The director's assistant dashed away, stumbling off the soundstage and tripping on loose wires.

Around them, the set showed an exotic nightclub, with white fake-adobe walls, potted tropical plants, and Arabic-looking squiggles on the pottery. The piano in the center of the stage, just in front of the bar, sat empty under the spotlight, waiting for the movie's star, Lance Chandler. The sound stage sweltered in the summer heat. The large standup fans had to be shut off before shooting; and the ceiling fans—nightclub props—stirred the cloud of cigarette smoke overhead into a gray whirlpool, making the extras cough even when they were supposed to keep silent.

Rino Derwell looked again at his gold wristwatch. He had bought it cheap from a man in an alley, but Derwell's pride would not allow him to admit he had been swindled even after it had promptly stopped working. Derwell didn't need it to tell him he was already well behind schedule, over budget, and out of patience.

It was going to take all day just to shoot a few seconds of finished footage. "God, I hate these transformation sequences. Why does the audience need to *see* everything? Have they no imagination?" he muttered. "Maybe I should just do romance movies? At least nobody wants to see everything *there*!"

"Oh, God! Please no! Not again! Not *NOW*!!!" Lance couldn't see the look of horror he hoped would show on his face.

"You must stop fidgeting, Mr. Lance. This will go much faster." Zoltan stepped back, large makeup brush in hand, inspecting his work. His heavy eastern European accent slurred out his words.

"Well I've got to practice my lines. This blasted makeup takes so blasted long that I forget my blasted lines by the time it comes to shoot. Was I supposed to say 'Don't let it happen *here*!' in that scene? Hand me the script."

"No, Mr. Lance. That line comes much later—it follows 'Oh no! I'm transforming!'" Zoltan smeared shadow under Lance's eyes. This would be just the first step in the transformation, but he still had to increase the highlights. Veins stood out on Zoltan's gnarled hands, but his fingers were rock steady with the fine detail.

"How do you know my lines?"

"You may call it gypsy intuition, Mr. Lance—or it may be because you have been saying them every morning before makeup for a week now. They have burned into my brain like a gypsy curse."

Lance glared at the wizened old man in his pale blue shirt and color-spattered smock. Zoltan's leathery fingers had a real instinct for makeup, for changing the appearance of any actor. But his craft took hours.

Lance Chandler had enough confidence in his own screen presence to carry any film, regardless of how silly the makeup made him look. His square jaw, fine physique, and clean-cut appearance made him the perfect model of the all-American hero in the WWII era flicks he was known for.

Lance took special pride in his performance in *Tarzan Versus the Third Reich*. Though he had few lines in the film, the animal rage on his face and his oiled and straining body had been enough to topple an entire regiment of Hitler's finest, including one of Rommel's desert vehicles. (Exactly why one of Rommel's desert vehicles had shown up in the middle of Africa's deepest jungles was a question only the scriptwriter could have answered.)

Craig Corwyn, U-Boat Smasher, to be released next month as the start of a new series, might make Lance a household name. Those stories centered on brave Craig Corwyn, who had a penchant for leaping off the deck of his Allied destroyer and swimming down to sink Nazi submarines with his bare hands, usually by opening the underwater hatches or just plucking out the rivets in the hull.

But none of those movies would compare to *Wolfman in Casablanca*. Bogart would be forgotten in a week. The timing for this film was just perfect; it had an emotional content Lance had not been able to bring into his earlier efforts. Strong and manly, with a dash of animal unpredictability and a heart of gold (not to mention unwavering in Allied sympathies).

The story concerned a troubled but patriotic were-wolf—him, Lance Chandler—who in his wanderings has found himself in German-occupied Casablanca. There he causes what havoc he can for the enemy, and he also meets Brigitte, a beautiful French resistance fighter vacationing in Morocco. Brigitte turns out to be a werewolf herself, Lance's true love. Even in the script, the final scene as the two of them howl on the rooftops above a conflagration of Nazi tanks and ruined artillery sent shivers down Lance's spine. If he could pull off this performance, Hitler himself would tremble in his grave.

Zoltan added spirit gum to Lance's cheeks and fore-head, humming as he worked. "You will please stop perspiring, Mr. Lance. I require a dry surface for this fine hair."

Lance slumped in the chair. Zoltan reminded him of the wicked old gypsy man in the movie, the one who had cursed his character to become a werewolf in the first place. "This blasted transformation sequence is going to take all day again, isn't it? And I don't even get to *act* after the first second or so! Lie still, add more hair, shoot a few frames, lie still, add more hair, shoot a few more frames. And it's so hot in the soundstage. The spirit gum burns and ruins my complexion. The fumes sting my eyes. The fake hair itches."

He winced his face into the practiced look of horror again. "Oh, God! Please no! Not again! Um...oh yeah—don't let it happen here!" Lance paused, then scowled. "Blast, that wasn't right. Would you hurry up, Zoltan! I'm already losing my lines. And I'm really tired of you dragging your feet—get moving!"

Zoltan tossed the makeup brush with a loud clink into its glass jar of solvent. He put his gnarled hands on his hips and glared at Lance. The smoldering gypsy fury in his dark eyes looked worse than anything Lance had seen on a movie villain's face.

"I lose my patience with you, Mr. Lance! It is gone! Poof! Now I must take a short cut. A special trick that only I know. It will take a minute, and it will make you a star forevermore! I guarantee that. You will no longer suffer my efforts—and I need not suffer you! The people at the new Frankenstein movie over on Lot Seventeen would appreciate my work, no doubt."

Lance blinked, amazed at the old gypsy's anger but ready to jump at any chance that would get him out of the makeup trailer sooner. He heard only the words "it will make you a star. I guarantee that."

"Well, do it then, Zoltan! I've got work to do. The great Lon Chaney never had to put up with all these delays. He did all his own makeup. My audiences are waiting to see the new meaning I can bring to the portrayal of the werewolf."

"You will never disappoint them, Mr. Lance."

Without further reply, Zoltan yanked at the fine hair he had already applied. "You no longer need this." Lance yowled as the patches came free of his skin. "That is a

very good sound you make, Mr. Lance. Very much like a werewolf."

Lance growled at him.

Zoltan rustled in a cardboard box in the corner of his cramped trailer, pulled out a dirty Mason jar, and unscrewed its rusty lid. Inside, a brown oily liquid swirled all by itself, spinning green flecks in internal currents. The old man stuck his fingers into the goop and brought them out dripping.

"What is—whoa, that smells like—" Lance tried to shrink away, but Zoltan slapped the goop onto his cheek and smeared it around.

"You cannot possibly know what this smells like, Mr. Lance, because you have no idea what I used to make it. You probably do not wish to know—then you would be even more upset at having it rubbed all over your face."

Zoltan reached into the jar again and brought out another handful, which he wiped across Lance's forehead. "Ugh! Did you get that from the lot cafeteria?" Lance felt his skin tingle, as if the liquid had begun to eat its way inside. "Ow! My complexion!"

"If it gives you pimples, you can always call them character marks, Mr. Lance. Every good actor has them."

Zoltan pulled his hand away. Lance saw that the old man's fingers were clean. "Finished. It has all absorbed right in." He screwed the cover of the jar back on and replaced it in the cardboard box.

Lance grabbed a small mirror, expecting to find his (soon-to-be) well-known expression covered with ugly brown, but he could see no sign of the makeup at all. "What happened to it? It still stinks."

"It is special makeup. It will work when it needs to."

The door flew open, and the red-faced director's assistant stood panting. "Lance, Mr. Derwell wants you on the set right now! Pronto! We've got to start shooting."

Zoltan nudged his shoulder. "I am finished with you, Mr. Lance."

Lance stood up, trying not to look perplexed so that Zoltan could have a laugh at his expense. "But I don't see any—"

The old gypsy wore a wicked grin on his lips. "You need not worry about it. I believe your expression is, 'Knock 'em dead.'"

Lance sat down at the nightclub piano and cracked his knuckles. The extras and other stars took their positions. Above the soundstage, he could hear men on the catwalks, positioning cool blue gels over the lights to simulate the full moon.

"*Now* are you ready, Lance?" the director said, fitting another cigarette into his mouth. "Or do you think maybe we should just take a coffee break for an hour or so?"

"That's not necessary, Mr. Derwell. I'm ready. Just give the word, see?" He growled for good measure.

"Places everyone!"

Lance ran his fingers over the piano keyboard, 'tickling the old ivories,' as real piano players called it. No sound came out. Lance couldn't play a note, of course, so the prop men had cut all the piano wires, holding the instrument in merciful silence no matter how enthusiastically Lance might bang on it. They would add the beautiful piano melody to the soundtrack during post-production.

"*Wolfman in Casablanca*, Scene Twenty-three, Take One." The clapboard cracked.

"Action!" Derwell called.

The klieg lights came on, pouring hot white illumination on the set. Lance stiffened at the piano, then began to hum and pretend to plink on the keys.

In this scene, the werewolf has taken a job as a piano player in a nightclub, where he has met Brigitte, the vacationing French resistance fighter. While playing "As Time Goes By," Lance's character looks up to see the full moon shining down through the nightclub's skylight. To keep from having to interrupt filming, Derwell had planned to shoot Lance from the back only as he played the piano, not showing his face until after he had supposedly started to transform. But now

Lance didn't appear to wear any makeup at all—he wondered what would happen when Derwell noticed, but he plunged into the performance nevertheless. That would be Zoltan's problem, not his.

At the appropriate point, Lance froze at the keyboard, forcing his fingers to tremble as he stared at them. On the soundtrack, the music would stop in mid-note. The false moonlight shone down on him. Lance formed his face into his best expression of abject horror.

"Oh, God! Please no! Not again! Don't let it happen *HERE*!!!" Lance clutched his chest, slid sideways, and did a graceful but dramatic topple off the piano bench.

On cue, one of the extras screamed. The bartender dropped a glass, which shattered on the tiles.

On the floor, Lance couldn't stop writhing. His own body felt as if it were being turned inside out. He had really learned how to bury himself in the role! His face and hands itched, burned. His fingers curled and clenched. It felt terrific. It felt *real* to him. He let out a moaning scream—and it took him a moment to realize it wasn't part of the act.

Off behind the cameras, Lance could see Rino Derwell jumping up and down with delight, jerking both his thumbs up in silent admiration for Lance's performance. "Cut!"

Lance tried to lie still. They would need to add the next layer of hair and makeup. Zoltan would come in and paste one of the latex appliances onto his eyebrows, darken his nails with shoe polish.

But Lance felt his own nails sharpening, curling into claws. Hair sprouted from the backs of his hands.

His cheeks tingled and burned. His ears felt sharp and stretched, protruding from the back of his head. His face tightened and elongated; his mouth filled with fangs.

"No, wait!" Derwell shouted at the cameraman. "Keep rolling! Keep rolling!"

"Look at that!" the director's assistant said.

Lance tried to say something, but he could only growl. His body tightened and felt ready to explode with anger. He found it difficult to concentrate, but some part of his mind knew what he had to do. After all, he had read the script.

Leaping up from the nightclub dance floor, Lance strained until his clothes ripped under his bulging lupine muscles. With a roar and a spray of saliva from his fang-filled jaws, he smashed the piano bench prop into kindling, knocking it aside.

Four of the extras screamed, even without their cues.

Lance heaved the giant, mute piano and smashed it onto its side. The severed piano wires jangled like a rasping old woman trying to sing. The bartender stood up and brought out a gun, firing four times in succession, but they were only theatrical blanks, and not silver blanks either. Lance knocked the gun aside, grabbed the bartender's arm, and hurled him across the stage, where he landed in a perfect stunt man's roll.

Lance Chandler stood under the klieg lights, in the pool of blue gel filtering through the skylight simulating the full moon. He bayed a beautiful wolf howl as everyone fled screaming from the stage.

"Cut! Cut! Lance, that's magnificent!" Derwell clapped his hands.

The klieg lights faded, leaving the wreckage under the normal room illumination. Lance felt all the energy drain out of him. His face rippled and contracted, his ears shrank back to normal. His throat remained sore from the long howl, but the fangs had vanished from his mouth. He brushed his hands to his cheeks, but found that all the abnormal hair had melted away.

Derwell ran onto the set and clapped him on the back. "That was *incredible!* Oscar-quality stuff!"

Old Zoltan stood at the edge of the set, smiling. His dark eyes glittered. Derwell turned to the gypsy and applauded him as well. "Marvelous, Zoltan! I can't believe it. How in the world did you do that?"

Zoltan shrugged, but his toothless grin grew wider. "Special makeup," he said. "Gypsy secret. I am pleased it worked out." He turned and shuffled toward the soundstage exit.

"Do you really think that was Oscar quality?" Lance asked.

The other actors treated Lance with a sort of awe, though a few tended to avoid him. The actress playing Brigitte kept fixing her eyes on him, raising her eyebrows in a suggestive expression. Derwell, having

shot a perfect take of the transformation scene he had thought would require more than a day, ordered the set crew to repair the werewolf-caused damage so they could shoot the big love scene, as a reward to everyone.

Zoltan said nothing to Lance as he added a heavy coat of pancake and sprayed his hair into place. Lance didn't know how the gypsy had worked the transformation, but he knew when not to ask questions. Derwell had said his performance was Oscar quality! He just grinned to himself and looked forward to the kissing scene with Brigitte. Lance always tried to make sure the kissing scenes required several takes. He enjoyed his work, and so (no doubt) did his female co-stars.

Zoltan added an extra-thick layer of dark-red lipstick to Brigitte's mouth, then applied a special wax sealing coat so that it wouldn't smear during the on-screen passion.

"All right you two," Derwell said, sitting back in his director's chair, "start gazing at each other and getting starry-eyed. Places everyone!"

Zoltan packed up his kit and left the soundstage. He said good-bye to the director, but Derwell waved him away in distraction.

Lance stared into Brigitte's eyes, then wiggled his eyebrows in what he hoped would be an irresistible invitation. He had few lines in this scene, only some low grunting and a mumbled "Yes, my love" during the kiss.

Brigitte gazed back at him, batting her eyelashes, melting him with her deep brown irises.

"*Wolfman in Casablanca*, Scene Thirty-nine, Take One."

Lance took a deep breath so he could make the kiss last longer.

"Action!" The klieg lights came on.

In silence, he and Brigitte gawked at each other. Romantic music would be playing on the soundtrack. They leaned closer to each other. She shuddered with her barely contained emotion. After an indrawn breath, she spoke in a sultry, sexy French accent. "You are the type of man I need. You are my soul-mate. Kiss me. I want you to kiss me."

He bent toward her. "Yes, my love."

His joints felt as if they had turned to ice water. His skin burned and tingled. He kissed her, pulling her close, feeling his passion rise to an uncontrollable pitch.

Brigitte jerked away. "Ow! Lance, you bit me!" She touched a spot of blood on her lip.

He felt his hands curl into claws, the nails turn hard and black. Hair began to sprout all over his body. He tried to stop the transformation, but he didn't know how. He stumbled backward. "Oh, God! Please no! Not again!"

"No, Lance—that's not your line!" Brigitte whispered to him.

His muscles bulged; his face stretched out into a long, sharp muzzle. His throat gurgled and growled. He looked around for something to smash. Brigitte screamed, though it wasn't in the script. Tossing her

aside, Lance uprooted one of the ornamental palms and hurled the clay pot to the other side of the stage.

"Cut!" the director called. "What the hell is going on here? It's just a simple scene!"

The klieg lights dimmed again. Lance felt the werewolf within him dissolving away, leaving him sweating and shaking and standing in clothes that had torn in several embarrassing places.

"Oh Lance, quit screwing around!" Derwell said. "Go to wardrobe and get some new clothes, for Christ's sake! Somebody, get a new plant and clean up that mess. Get First Aid to fix Brigitte's lip here. Come on, people!" Derwell shook his head.

Lance skipped going to wardrobe and went to Zoltan's makeup trailer instead. He didn't know how he was going to discuss this with the gypsy, but if all else failed he could just knock the old man flat with a good roundhouse punch, in the style of Craig Corwyn, U-Boat Smasher.

When he pounded on the flimsy door, though, it swung open by itself. A small sign hung by a string from the doorknob. In Zoltan's scrawling handwriting, it said, "FAREWELL, MY COMPANIONS. TIME TO MOVE ON. GYPSY BLOOD CALLS."

Lance stepped inside. "All right, Zoltan. I know you're in here!"

But he knew no such thing, and the cramped trailer proved to be empty indeed. Many of the bottles had been removed from the shelves, the brushes, the latex prosthetics all packed and taken. Zoltan had also carried away the old cardboard box from the corner, the one containing the jar of special makeup for Lance.

In the makeup chair, Lance found a single sheet of paper that had been left for him. He picked it up and stared down at it, moving his lips as he read.

"Mr. Lance,

"My homemade concoction may eventually wear off, as soon as you learn a little more patience. Or it may not. I cannot tell. I have always been afraid to use my special makeup, until I met you.

"Do not try to find me. I have gone with the crew of *Frankenstein of the Farmlands* to shoot on location in Iowa. I will be gone for some time. Director Derwell asked me to leave, to save him time and money. Worry not, though, Mr. Lance. You no longer need any makeup from me.

"I promised you would become a star. Now, every time the glow of the klieg lights strikes your face, you will transform into a werewolf. You will doubtless be in every single werewolf movie produced from now on. How can they refuse?

"P.S. You should hope that werewolves are not just a passing fad! You know how fickle audiences can be."

Lance Chandler crumpled the note, then straightened it again so he could tear it into shreds, but he didn't need any werewolf anger to snarl this time.

He stared around the empty makeup trailer, feeling his career shatter around him. There would be no more Tarzan roles, no thrilling adventures of Craig Corwyn. His hopes, his dreams were ruined, and his cry of anguish sounded like a mournful wolf's howl.

"I've been typecast!"

CAST AND CREW

ABOUT THE CAST

MARIO ACEVEDO is a national bestselling author of speculative fiction and has won an International Latino Book Award and a Colorado Book Award. His work has appeared in numerous anthologies to include *A Fistful of Dinosaurs, Straight Outta Deadwood*, and *Blood Business*. For 2020, he has short fiction in the forthcoming anthologies, *Psi-Wars* and *It Came from the Multiplex*, and a Western novel, *Luther, Wyoming*. Mario serves on the faculty of the Regis University Mile-High MFA program and Lighthouse Writers Workshops.

KEVIN J. ANDERSON is the author of more than 165 novels, 56 of which have been national or international bestsellers. He has written novels in the *Dune, Star Wars*, and *X-Files* universes as well as his own original novels *Spine of the Dragon*, the Dan Shamble, Zombie P.I. series, *The Saga of Seven Suns*, and two steampunk fantasy adventure novels with Neil Peart, legendary drummer and lyricist from Rush.

PAUL CAMPION grew up in the 80s on a steady diet of horror films. He worked in the film industry as a visual effects artist on iconic movie monsters such as the Balrog, Fellbeast and Shelob in Peter Jackson's *The Lord of the Rings* trilogy. He directed the award-winning short films *Night of the Hell Hamsters*, *Eel Girl* and *The Naughty List*, all of which have screened at major genre film festivals around the world. His feature film directorial debut, *The Devil's Rock*—a WWII occult horror movie, showcased makeup effects by Oscar-winning studio Weta Workshop and so much fake blood it permanently stained the floor of the set red. Paul is in post-production on his fourth short film, *Back in Business*, starring Matthew Kelly, and is in development on his second horror feature film.

K. NICOLE DAVIS received her MFA in Creative Writing from the University of Colorado-Boulder. She loves living in, exploring, and writing Colorado.

KEVIN DILMORE has teamed with author and best pal Dayton Ward for nearly twenty years on novels, shorter fiction and other writings chiefly in the *Star Trek* universe. As a senior writer for Hallmark Cards, Kevin has helped create books, Keepsake Ornaments, greeting cards and other products featuring characters from DC Comics, Marvel Comics, *Star Trek*, *Star Wars*, and other properties. He is a content approver for the recent Rainbow Brite comics series by Dynamite Entertainment. A contributor to publications including *The Village Voice*, *Amazing Stories*, *Star Trek Commu-*

nicator, and *Famous Monsters of Filmland,* he lives in Overland Park, Kansas.

SEAN EADS is a writer and librarian living in Colorado. His first novel, *The Survivors,* was a finalist for the Lambda Literary Award. His third novel, *Lord Byron's Prophecy,* was a finalist for the Shirley Jackson Award and the Colorado Book Award. His short stories have appeared in various anthologies.

KEITH FERRELL was the author of a dozen or so books, fiction and nonfiction, as well as over 1,000 magazine and encyclopedia articles and essays. He was co-author, with Brad Meltzer, of the *New York Times* bestseller *History Decoded.* From 1990 to 1996 he was editor-in-chief of *OMNI Magazine.* His short fiction has appeared in *Asimov's, Black Mist, Millennium 300, Nightmares Unhinged, Cyber World,* among others. His website is *www.keithferrellwriter.com.*

ORRIN GREY is a skeleton who likes monsters and the author of a number of spooky books. His stories have been published in dozens of anthologies, including Ellen Datlow's *Best Horror of the Year,* and he regularly writes about film for places like *Signal Horizon* and *Unwinnable,* to name just a few. You can find him online at *www.orringrey.com.*

WARREN HAMMOND has authored several science fiction novels, quite a few short stories, and a graphic novel. His 2012 novel, *KOP Killer*, won the Colorado Book Award for best mystery. His latest series, Denver Moon, is co-written with Joshua Viola. He is also chief intoxicologist and co-host of the Critiki Party podcast.

ANGIE HODAPP is the Director of Literary Development at Nelson Literary Agency. She holds a BA in English and secondary education and an MA in English and communication development, and she is a graduate of the Denver Publishing Institute at the University of Denver. She has worked in publishing and professional writing and editing for the better part of the last two decades, and in addition to writing, she loves helping authors hone their craft and learn about the ever-changing business of publishing.

GARY JONAS is the author of too many books, including twelve novels about paranormal investigator Jonathan Shade, five about magically-engineered assassin Kelly Chan, four about the Half-Assed Wizard, and various stand-alone titles. He's had a couple of screenplays optioned in Hollywood, and worked on a few short films and features as a writer, producer, and even an actor...well, an extra, really, but he did those roles with such style that nobody even noticed. Visit him online at *www.garyjonasbooks.com*.

STEPHEN GRAHAM JONES is the author of sixteen and a half novels, six story collections, a couple of novellas, and a couple of one-shot comic books. Most recent are *Mapping the Interior* and *My Hero*. Next are *The Only Good Indians* and *Night of the Mannequins*. Stephen lives and teaches in Boulder, Colorado.

BETTY ROCKSTEADY creeps and crawls around a small town in Canada, watching 20s cartoons and introducing herself to stray cats. Her fiction explores body horror, weird sex and trauma, diving into the deepest darkest places she can go. Her debut collection of short fiction *In Dreams We Rot* is a nightmarish dive into neurosis and as sickening as a fever dream. Her cosmic sex horror novella *Writhing Skies* was the winner of the This Is Horror Awards' Novella of the Year 2018. Find out more at *www.bettyrocksteady.com* or by following Betty Rocksteady on Facebook or Twitter.

STEVE RASNIC TEM is a past winner of the World Fantasy, Bram Stoker, and British Fantasy Awards. He has published over 450 short stories, with some of his best collected in *Figures Unseen: Selected Stories* (Valancourt). His latest book is *The Night Doctor and Other Tales* (Centipede Press).

DAYTON WARD is a *New York Times* bestselling author or co-author of nearly forty novels and novellas, often working with his best friend, Kevin Dilmore. His short fiction has appeared in more than twenty anthologies and he's written for publications such as *NCO Journal, Kansas City Voices, Famous Monsters of Filmland, Star Trek Magazine* and *Star Trek Communicator* as well as the websites *Tor.com, StarTrek.com,* and *Syfy.com.* Though he lives in Kansas City with his wife and two daughters, Dayton is a Florida native and still maintains a torrid long-distance romance with his beloved Tampa Bay Buccaneers. Find him on the web at *www.daytonward.com.*

ALVARO ZINOS-AMARO is a Hugo and Locus Award finalist who has published some forty stories and over one hundred reviews, essays and interviews in venues like *Clarkesworld, Asimov's, Analog, Lightspeed, Tor.com, Locus, Beneath Ceaseless Skies, Nature, Strange Horizons, The Los Angeles Review of Books,* and anthologies such as *The Year's Best Science Fiction & Fantasy 2016, Cyber World, Humanity 2.0, Blood Business, This Way to the End Times, Shades Within Us, The Unquiet Dreamer,* and *Nox Pareidolia.*

ABOUT THE SPECIAL EFFECTS TEAM

AARON LOVETT's work has been featured by Dark Horse Comics and published in *Spectrum 22* and *24.* His *Nightmares Unhinged* (Hex Publishers) cover art was licensed by AMC for their hit TV show *Fear the*

Walking Dead. You can see his most recent character art in *Monster Train*, the upcoming PC game from Shiny Shoe and Good Shepherd Entertainment. His art can also be found in various other video games, books and comics. You can view his portfolio at *www.artstation.com/adlovett*. He paints from a dark corner in Denver, Colorado.

AJ NAZZARO is a freelance illustrator and concept artist living in Denver, Colorado. He is a lifelong gamer and has worked in the trading card and video game industry for almost ten years. After working with Wizards of the Coast on the game *Kaijudo*, he began creating artwork for *Hearthstone* including thirteen expansions and over sixty cards. AJ also contributes artwork to two other Blizzard Entertainment titles, *Overwatch* and *Heroes of the Storm*.

XANDER SMITH began drawing as soon as he was old enough to pick up a pencil. Art has been his lifelong passion and led to studies at the Gnomon School of Visual Effects and Concept Design Academy in Los Angeles, eventually paving his way to a career in Hollywood as a concept artist. His father's chance conversation with actress Heather Langenkamp at a *Star Trek* convention led to Xander's first job with AFX Studio illustrating the Red Devil in Ryan Murphy's *Scream Queens*. Since then, he's developed concept art and costumes for five seasons of *American Horror Story*. Xander's work has also appeared in the feature films *The Greatest Showman*, *Aquaman* and *Godzilla vs. Kong*. He has worked for 21st Century Fox, Alliance Studio, Ironhead Studio, Gentle Giant Studios, Jim Henson Studios, Studio ADI and Digital Domain. He is currently the lead artist at Neon Evolution. His website is *www.artstation.com/xandersmith*.

ABOUT THE PRODUCERS

BRET SMITH retired from IBM after thirty-four years as a program manager. He's a lifelong *Star Trek* fan and loves all things pop culture. He met his wife **JEANNI SMITH** on a blind date while she was attending the University of Arizona for her BFA. They've been happily married for over thirty years, attending conventions together since the 80s—their most beloved decade—including over fourteen San Diego Comic-Cons. They raised two artistic sons, Xander—a successful Hollywood artist, and Cameron—a multi-talented musician. Today, when Jeanni isn't busy working as an antiques dealer, she and Bret are focused on their responsibilities as co-founders of the Colorado Festival of Horror, which features the passion project you're holding in your hands now.

ABOUT THE DIRECTOR

JOSHUA VIOLA is a four-time Colorado Book Award finalist and co-author of the Denver Moon series with Warren Hammond. His comic book collection, *Denver Moon: Metamorphosis*, was included on the 2018 Bram Stoker Award Preliminary Ballot for Superior Achievement in a Graphic Novel. He edited the *Denver Post* #1 bestselling anthology, *Nightmares Unhinged*, and co-edited *Cyber World*—named one of the best science fiction anthologies of 2016 by Barnes & Noble. His fiction has appeared in numerous anthologies, *Birdy* magazine, and on *Tor.com*. He is owner and chief editor of Hex Publishers.

ACKNOWLEDGMENTS

CPSIA information can be obtained
at www.ICGtesting.com
Printed in the USA
LVHW022320150920
666084LV00005B/946